The Lorette Wilmot Library
Nazareth College of Rochester

Walker's Crossing

BOOKS BY PHYLLIS REYNOLDS NAYLOR

Witch's Sister

Witch Water

The Witch Herself

Walking Through the Dark

How I Came to Be a Writer

How Lazy Can You Get?

Eddie, Incorporated

All Because I'm Older

Shadows on the Wall

Faces in the Water

Footprints at the Window

The Boy with the Helium Head

A String of Chances

The Solomon System

The Mad Gasser of Bessledorf Street

Night Cry

Old Sadie and the Christmas Bear

The Dark of the Tunnel

The Agony of Alice

The Keeper

The Bodies in the Bessledorf Hotel

The Year of the Gopher

Beetles, Lightly Toasted

Maudie in the Middle

One of the Third Grade Thonkers

Alice in Rapture, Sort Of

Keeping a Christmas Secret

Bernie and the Bessledorf Ghost

Send No Blessings

Reluctantly Alice

King of the Playground

Shiloh

All but Alice

Josie's Troubles

The Grand Escape

Alice in April

The Face in the Bessledorf Funeral
Parlor

Alice In-Between

The Fear Place

Alice the Brave

Being Danny's Dog

Ice

The Bomb in the Bessledorf Bus Depot

Alice in Lace

Shiloh Season

Ducks Disappearing

Outrageously Alice

The Healing of Texas Jake

I Can't Take You Anywhere

Saving Shiloh

The Treasure of Bessledorf Hill

Achingly Alice

Danny's Desert Rats

Sang Spell

Sweet Strawberries

Alice on the Outside

Walker's Crossing

PHYLLIS REYNOLDS NAYLOR

Walker's Crossing

A JEAN KARL BOOK

ATHENEUM BOOKS FOR YOUNG READERS

SPECIAL THANKS TO CHUCK REED, BLM WYOMING, WHO MADE
SUGGESTIONS FOR THIS BOOK, AND TO THE SOUTHERN POVERTY LAW
CENTER FOR THE INFORMATION THAT THEY SUPPLIED

Atheneum Books for Young Readers
An imprint of Simon & Schuster Children's Publishing Division
1230 Avenue of the Americas
New York, New York 10020
Book design by Angela Carlino
The text of this book is set in Apollo.
Printed in the United States of America
10 9 8 7 6 5 4 3
Library of Congress Cataloging-in-Publication Data
Naylor, Phyllis Reynolds.
Walker's Crossing / Phyllis Reynolds Naylor.
p. cm. "A Jean Karl Book."
Summary: While living on his family's ranch in Wyoming where he hopes to
someday be a cowboy, Ryan faces conflicts with his older brother, who
becomes involved in a militia movement.
ISBN 0-689-82939-6
[1. Ranch life—Wyoming—Fiction. 2. Cowboys—Fiction.
3. Brothers—Fiction. 4. Prejudices—Fiction. 5. Militia movements—Fiction.
6. Wyoming—Fiction.] I. Title.
PZ7.N24Wai 1999 [Fic]—dc21 98-50217

To our sons, Jeffrey and Michael

One

A slice of moon, white as paper, slipped behind the clouds that rolled across the huge gray bowl of sky.

"Owl-ooo!"

The howl split the air, and the clouds seemed to jump.

Ryan Walker stepped out from behind the scrub pines, breathing hard, and gave the wolf howl again.

A window rose in the small frame house. Matt Sheldon replied with a low whistle, then disappeared from view, and Ryan went to the porch to wait. It didn't pay to come knocking at the Sheldons' lonely house after dark. If you were going to be roaming around out there, Richard Sheldon, Matt's father, wanted to know. But sometimes Ryan got restless and just had to move. He'd go outside and run, and the Sheldons' house, being four miles off, seemed only two miles by Ryan's legs. More often than not, he'd end up there.

He sat down on the steps, long legs folding under him like a stork's, the cold seeping through his jeans, and took off his wide-brimmed hat, stained with the sweat of several summers. He was six foot one already, and taller than anyone his age. Taller than most of his teachers, even, and growing still. Yet he was pole-bean skinny, and all the food in the world went into height, it seemed.

You're off the charts, that's for sure, but basically you're healthy, so don't let it get to you, the doctor had said when Ryan had gone in last year with strep throat.

Straight ahead, the jagged mountains rose up steep and dark against the purple sky. Ryan's dad, Lon Walker, was caretaker for the Saddlebow Ranch, and they lived in a house on the property. Matt had moved up with his family from California three years ago, and his dad had bought this old place next to the Saddlebow.

Matt came out on the porch in a new wool jacket. "That howl of yours sounds more like a sick Comanche." He grinned.

"Heck, Comanches could sound like any animal at all," Ryan said. "Where'd you get the jacket?"

"Truck stop store. Birthday present. Hasn't been cold enough to wear to school yet." Matt sat down beside him on the top step. "What's up?"

"Just out running."

Giving Ryan a nudge, Matt pulled something out of a pocket. "Want some?"

In the near dark, Ryan put out his hand and felt something light touch his palm. He brought it to his nostrils and sniffed. "Tobacco?" he asked.

"Red Man." Matt showed the pack. "It was in the right pocket. I'll bet someone was trying the jacket on and forgot he put it in there."

"I'll bet some kid lifted a pack, then chickened out and dropped it in a jacket," guessed Ryan, handing it back. "T. P. keeps an eye on things like that." He rubbed his hand on his pant leg to wipe off the tobacco scent. "Mom would kill me. Her dad died from cancer of the jaw."

Matt bit off a plug, chewed for a minute or two, then spit. He tossed the pack to Ryan. "Give it to your brother, then."

"Mom doesn't like him to chew, either."

"I figure when you're nineteen you can do whatever you want," Matt told him.

The door suddenly opened behind them.

"Matt, who's out there?" A man's voice. Sharp sounding.

"Just Ryan."

Mr. Sheldon appeared in the doorway, staring hard through the darkness. He was a wiry man, lean as a greyhound, his plaid shirt covering the denim he wore over his tee. "Well, what you doing, you can't come inside?"

"Just talking, Dad," Matt said.

"I was out running," Ryan told him. "Stopped by to cool off."

"Oh. Okay, then," Mr. Sheldon said, and went back inside.

"What's he *think* we do out here?" Ryan asked, curious. "Drugs? Dance around naked or something?"

Matt laughed. "It's just his way."

The Sheldons believed in home-schooling their kids, but last year they'd let Matt start middle school as an experiment. *You can't judge the steel if it's never been tested,* Matt's father had said. Ryan wasn't sure just what kind of testing that would be, because as soon as Matt started school, the girls called him "cute." And "cute," it had seemed to Ryan, studying his friend, would get you about anything you wanted.

The boys sat watching Ryan's dogs romp and tussle about the yard. Matt's face was squarely built; Ryan's had more of an egg shape. They both had brown hair, but Matt's eyes were blue, Ryan's brown, and Ryan was taller by almost a foot. The air felt like September, all right. There were places in the country where September felt like July, but here in Wyoming, nestled between mountains, when fall came you knew it.

"What'cha doing tomorrow?" Matt asked.

"I don't know. Give the dogs a bath, maybe. They stink something awful. Work for Hank, of course."

"He ever going to start paying you?"

"I never asked. Heck, I'd pay *him* just to let me go up with the cattle next summer."

"That's crazy."

"Only thing in this world I ever really wanted," Ryan told him.

"What you doing Sunday, then?"

"Ride over to Teepee's, I guess. Work on that report for history."

Matt hunched his shoulders and thrust each hand up the opposite sleeve of his jacket. "I noticed you teamed up with Barry on that report. Why didn't you go in with me?"

"'Cause I wanted to do American Indians. Didn't want to write about rocks."

"Rocks, you get to do gold mines," Matt said.

"Indians, you get to do Comanches." Ryan smiled. "Man, I sure wish you'd get a phone. Have to come all the way over here every time I want to talk to you."

"Well, you'll never talk Dad into getting one. Once they get your number, he says, they'll learn everything there is to know about you."

"Who's 'they'?"

Matt shrugged. "Government spies."

"You're nuts." Ryan gave a small laugh and shifted impatiently on the steps. Matt had talked like this before, and it was the only time he was ever serious. It didn't do to joke with Matt about his dad.

"He knows what he's talking about," Matt said.

Ryan leaned forward so far that his chin rested on his knees; he tried to determine how much he could see to the right or left without moving his head. Hardly anything at all because it was getting so dark. All they had was the light from the window.

"Well, they can watch me all they want, because right now I've got the most boring life in the world," he said at last. "I wish I lived over at Hank's, that's what I wish."

But Matt continued: "Won't be so boring if they *do* come around here. And you know what else? About the new guy? Barry?"

"What?"

"Dad says his dad's probably one of 'em."

"Oh, Matt, now you're *really* talking nuts."

"You'll see. We never had a Jew-boy around here before."

"How do you know he's Jewish?"

"Dubinsky! Sounds like a Jew name to me."

Ryan shrugged and stood up. "Maybe. Listen, I got to get home." He whistled, and the two dogs—a Border collie and a kelpie—came angling over, ready to start the homeward trek. "See you at Teepee's?"

"Probably," said Matt.

Ryan started off across the frosty ground, his boots crunching on the sagebrush. It was cold here at night, but would heat up quickly in the daytime. His toes were always the first to go numb.

"Heck, your blood's got such a long way to travel that by the time it gets to your feet, it's gone cold," his father used to joke.

He thought again about what Matt had said about

Barry Dubinsky's dad being a government spy. He didn't believe half the stuff Matt told him—Matt had an imagination bigger than the Grand Canyon—but sometimes he was right. You just didn't know *which* times, was all.

Ryan was thinking about what had happened on the first day of school a week ago, after he'd boarded the bus. He'd high-fived a couple of friends he hadn't seen since the start of summer vacation, and had taken a seat halfway back.

"Hey, Lighthouse! How you doin'?" had come a call, not unfriendly.

He'd grinned.

"Hi, Flagpole!" the calls had continued.

"Hey, Shorty!" they'd teased.

"Hey, Legs!"

"Geez, Ryan! You grow another foot?"

All over the bus, people had called out to each other, catching up on news, and it wasn't till he'd heard someone ask, "Who's the new guy?" that he'd noticed the short boy with the dark hair sitting two rows behind the driver.

The kid had the studied casualness of a newcomer, dressed in the sort of nondescript jeans and running shoes that invite no comment, his backpack nothing special, no insignia on his jacket.

Just let me fade into the woodwork, his clothes had seemed to say. *Don't single me out.*

"What's your name?" someone had called.

The guy in the denim jacket had stared straight ahead.

"Hey, Levine!" came another voice.

A silence, then a titter. No answer.

"Weinstein? Goldfarb?" the voice had continued, and somebody laughed.

"Shut up, Kevin," said someone.

"I'm just trying to be friendly," Kevin had said. "Hey! Hey, you in the denim jacket. What's your name?"

When it was obvious they were speaking to him, the short guy had turned halfway around in his seat. "Hi," he'd said, smiling faintly. "Barry Dubinsky."

"Hi, Barry," a girl had called.

"Dubinsky?" Then it was Matt talking. "That a Yiddie name, or what?"

"Oh, Matt . . . !" somebody scolded.

Barry had faced forward again, smile fading.

Ryan didn't think Barry looked much different from anyone else. Hair was a little darker, maybe, but not as dark as Sheila Harrison's. Nose a little straighter? Hard to tell.

There was something about the slump of the guy's shoulders that had caused a familiar ache in Ryan's gut. He knew how it felt to be odd man out, not knowing what was coming next. Barry would just have to get used to teasing, though. *He* had.

In third grade, a classmate had complained that Ryan's knees dug into him from behind, seated as they'd been in the ancient regulation desks that were bolted in rows to the floor. In fourth, his knees hadn't fit under the desks at all, so the janitor had salvaged an old teacher's desk—a hideous thing of yellow oak—and placed it at the back of the room. There Ryan had sat, like some oversized beast, his feet resting one on top the other in his leather boots. The desk had followed him into the fifth-grade classroom, and when he entered sixth, Ryan found that the janitor had moved the desk over to the middle school wing as well. He'd put it there in Ryan's homeroom, as though Ryan were supposed to drag it with him from class to class. Ryan had refused to sit at it this time—sat *on* it, actually, while the teacher made the morning announcements; the teacher never cared.

When he'd started school this year, in seventh, the desk was gone—exiled at last to the basement. Ryan had hoped somehow to feel different sitting with the others, but he didn't. He sat sprawled awkwardly in the third row, like the village freak, legs taking up too much space, eyes on the window and the wild Wyoming sky.

It took longer to go the four miles home again than it did to get to the Sheldons' because Ryan walked this time. He made fists of his fingers in both pockets to keep them warm, and wished the collie didn't walk so close to him—like a cat, almost—yet had to admit it helped keep his legs warm. Sitting on the porch with Matt, he'd managed to get chilled through. Being thin as a yardstick, the cold got to him sooner than anyone he knew: no insulation.

He took a shortcut across the field of timothy grass that the Saddlebow grew for hay, but it was still some time before he saw the light from his own house. *Walker's Crossing,* they called it, because the man who had lived on that property years ago, before the Saddlebow bought it up, had built a little makeshift bridge over the river back there and charged travelers to go across. *Whittaker's Crossing,* folks called it then, and when Ryan's father became a cow boss and they moved into the house, they changed the name. Gil did, anyway. Burned the words *Walker's Crossing* into a log they used as a cross-beam between two poles over the entrance of the driveway. He put the apostrophe in the wrong place, though. Looked as though the land belonged to only one Walker. Didn't belong to any of them, really, it belonged to the Saddlebow, but it was home to all six.

Of course, it was sort of a joke out here in the valley. The bridge was long gone, for one thing, and so, sometimes, was the water. You drove under that cross-beam, you'd think you were entering a real ranch, but Walker's Crossing itself was only one small piece of the Saddlebow. All it had was the house, a barn, some sheds, six head of cattle, including the bull, three horses, plus two dogs, seven cats, some laying hens, and whatever wild or friendly animal wandered in from time to time, stayed a few days, and moved on.

Still, Ryan liked walking between those two poles when he came home, liked seeing *Walker's Crossing* above the entrance to the long dirt lane leading up to the house, as though this was someplace important, someplace special.

Tonight, though, he'd come by way of the cottonwood grove that separated the timothy grass from the house, and was about twenty feet from the driveway when he stopped, because a car with its headlights off was coming slowly down the lane.

Standing there in the September chill, Ryan tried to make out whose car it was, who was in it. But the sky was too dark now.

When they get to the end of the drive, they'll realize they don't have their lights on, he thought.

But the car pulled out onto the narrow country road and went some distance before Ryan saw the taillights come on, slowly disappearing around the bend.

Two

The two-story house was larger than the Sheldons', but twice as drafty. Mother always said that if the Air Force ever wanted a wind tunnel, they were welcome to this one. If you looked either west or east, you saw mountains. If you looked to the north, mountains and river. The view to the south was of the sprawling prairie.

Doris Walker was a tall, squarely built woman with red hair turning gray at the temples. She wore it shoulder-length, which looked nice, Ryan thought, when it was clean and brushed, but he didn't like it raggedy. Seemed to pull her face down.

She was always in jeans except for the hottest days of summer, when she put on shorts and a T-shirt. Now, when Ryan walked in, she was nudging a cat off a chair so she could watch the TV.

"Where *you* been?" she asked when he entered, the dogs trotting in happily behind him, but he hardly ever bothered to answer because she never listened, anyway. It was more a greeting than a question. An acknowledgment. When you were the second son in a family, three of the kids boys, and your ma liked the oldest best, you could more or less go where you wanted and she wouldn't even know you were gone.

Charlene, who was sixteen, sat on the sofa with four-year-old Freddy, eating a bowl of ice cream. She was built like her mother, but shorter, and had a round face with cheeks that puffed out like crab apples when she smiled, a dimple in the left. The only thing she and Ryan had in common was their skin, which, like their dad's, tanned well in the summer.

Freddy was in his pajamas already. "Ryan, want some ice cream?" he chirped.

"Can't. It's gone. We finished it off," Charlene told him, eyes on the TV.

Ryan didn't much care, actually, because he was too cold to enjoy it.

"Who was just here?" he asked his father, who was watching the screen disinterestedly.

"What d'ya mean? Nobody."

"I saw a car leaving as I came in."

"Must have got the wrong place," Mother said. "Wasn't anybody up to the door."

Ryan leaned over to pick up the sleepy cat who had

been displaced, and the pack of Red Man fell out of his jacket pocket onto the floor. Doris Walker saw it first.

"What the dickens is *that?*"

Ryan picked it up and handed it to her. "Matt got himself a new jacket at Teepee's and found this in the pocket," he said.

"So what *you* doin' with it?"

"He said give it to Gil."

"Boy, I ever see this stuff in your mouth, I'll whip you from here to Sunday," Mother said, dropping it into the wastebasket. "You know what Red Man did to Dad."

"You don't have to worry about me," said Ryan. The family remembered all too well the festering sore that ate right through Gramp's cheek, the way half his face was removed to save him, and still he died. Gil, of course, went on chewing. So did half the guys Ryan's age.

"Anybody can talk you into anything," Mother continued. "Just mention something, and Ryan's got to try it."

Her remark stung. "That's not true," Ryan said. She always did that. Took one little piece of fact and stretched it into a whole coat to cover you, just because Matt had talked him into riding a colt once, and he almost got stomped to death.

He sat down on a chair in the corner, cradling the cat in his arms. The striped tabby yawned and stretched, extending and retracting its claws, then sleepily closed its yellow eyes again, and the legs went limp.

14

Ryan watched his dad watching the TV. Lon Walker's eyes were a million miles away, it seemed. Freddy had just been born when their dad was thrown from a horse and broke two bones in his back. Broke his leg and a couple of ribs as well. And he seemed to know, when he came home from the hospital, that he'd never be cow boss again. That he might never ride again, in fact. And he hadn't. Ryan knew without asking that his dad was in constant pain. He never said so, but his whole disposition had changed. The family knew when to tread easy around him. It was a long step down from cow boss to caretaker, and this was not the way Lon Walker had envisioned his life. Not like this at all.

At the end of the local news, there was a listing of all the real estate sales that had taken place that week in the county. Ryan's parents always paid attention to the slow scrolling of names on the screen. Everyone did. It was a way to stay connected, spread out as they were over sagebrush country.

"You see that one?" asked Mother. "Huang. That's Oriental, isn't it?"

They watched some more.

"Look at that!" said Dad. "Jim Cobb sold his place for one hundred forty-seven thousand dollars. Thought he'd get more'n that, all that timber."

"Sold to a Chinaman, I'll bet," said Mother. "Oriental or Jew, one or the other. Gettin' so many slant-eyes out here, our kids'll be learning Chinese in school."

"What if it *was* a Chinaman?" Freddy asked.

"They'd take over, that's what," said Mother. "This land was built by folks like us—Walkers, Coopers, Higgins, Bates. . . . You start letting the immigrants buy up land, it won't be the America we knew."

Ryan thought about that awhile and continued stroking the cat, whose purr vibrated against the crook of his arm. "Mr. Phillips said we were all immigrants once—all but the Indians," he said, remembering something the new teacher had mentioned just that morning to start off their history project on the American West.

"One time, yes. But that was a long time ago before the country was civilized, and it's full up now. Somebody forgot to put up the 'No Vacancy' sign," said Dad, one corner of his wide mouth tilting slightly upward. "United States oughtn't to let any more in until it can do right by the ones it's got."

Well, that made sense to Ryan. Let Mexicans stay in their own country, the Japs in theirs. It wasn't as though the U.S. was unexplored—people coming in from all over the place to claim it.

Music drifted up from the basement. Ryan and Freddy shared one of the three bedrooms upstairs, but Gil got the whole basement to himself. He had his boom box next to his bed, a huge Confederate flag covering one wall, his posters and stuff on another.

Ryan figured that if Gil ever left home—got married or something—he could take over the basement himself. Hang up his own pictures. Line one whole wall with shelves for all the stuff he collected, mostly old ranch and rodeo stuff—a belt buckle worn by Ty Murray; a rope that belonged to Montie Montana; an old-time lantern; a miniature statue of Casey Tibbs riding his bronc Necktie; a branding iron; spurs (lots of them); photos of famous calf ropers, Indian riders, steer wrestlers, trick riders, bulldoggers, barrel racers, saddle bronc riders, and wranglers; a couple of old bullets; and his most prized possession of all, a roundish rock that his science teacher told him was probably a dinosaur dropping from the Jurassic period. It had been a big hit at school the year before. He'd passed it around the room so that everyone could say they'd touched dinosaur dung. The only girl who hadn't made a face was Sheila, and Ryan liked that about her.

Ryan lived for Saturdays. He was *made* for Saturdays. Early on a Saturday morning, the dark sky faintly tinted with pink and gold, he was usually on his way to the ranch foreman's house. With every step, the tension of the school week seemed to lessen, his mood to lighten, the isolation he felt in the classroom to fade away, as though he were going home—as if *this* were home—the place where he belonged.

The foreman, Hank Floyd, used to be called manager back when the Saddlebow was a lot bigger, and it took twice as many men to run it. But now that the owners had sold some of it off, Hank took over as foreman, and he and Dennis Shay, who used to be boss of one of the cow crews and was now boss of the *only* cow crew, pretty much ran the ranch themselves. Except for a little man called Moe, who managed the feedlot, they—along with Ryan's dad—were the only employees who worked the Saddlebow full time.

Hank Floyd's house was one of four buildings hidden among some trees. There were several pickups in the front yard, and the smell of coffee ("spur juice," the cowboys called it) filled the air.

"Here comes Shorty," a rawboned man said, who was nearly as tall and lean as Ryan, which made it okay. "How ya doin', Ryan?" Dennis Shay's weathered face crinkled around the eyes as he looked Ryan's way.

"Fine. How 'bout you?"

"Good as these fifty-two-year-old bones will let me," Dennis replied, following the other cowhands inside, their spurs clinking.

"You don't look fifty-two," Ryan told him.

"Maybe not, but sometimes I feel nine days older'n God, and that's the truth."

The men, Ryan included, left their hats in a pile in a corner of the living room, then gathered in the kitchen where Debbie, Hank Floyd's wife, was cooking breakfast for them all. The big farm table, surrounded with mismatched chairs, already held steaming platters of eggs and bacon, biscuits, grits, and fried potatoes, and the men sat down and began to eat. Hank, a blue kerchief around his neck, shuffled about, seeing that the coffee pot was on the table, waiting till all the men had filled their plates, then helping himself last. His forehead was white where the sun never reached when he was wearing his Stetson, and he had a long handlebar mustache that was still dark brown, a memory of the color his hair had once been.

There was little talk during breakfast. Moe, shortest of the men at five foot one, sat with the heels of his boots hooked over the rung of his chair. The cowboys went about the task of stoking up as studiously as they'd harness a horse. Then, one by one, they'd tell Debbie Floyd they enjoyed it, carry their plates to the sink, and go outside. They'd stand on the porch in their leather chaps and pass around a tin of Copenhagen—their "snoose," they called it—spitting long streams of brown tobacco juice over the rail. Ryan didn't know the last names of anybody except Dennis and Hank and Moe. You'd almost think the other men didn't have last names. They were just Sparkie or Jiggs or Clyde or Pete, cowboys who drifted in and out, season to season, depending on where they could find work. Sparkie and Clyde, though, were up in the Bighorns right now with the cattle.

"Tell Sparkie he still owes me twenty," burly Jiggs said to Dennis Shay. "You ever win at cards with that son-of-a-gun, it'll take you a year to collect."

The other men laughed. It was then that Ryan noticed the duffel bags sitting on the steps, the pickup loading at the side of the house.

"You going up to get the herd?" he asked Dennis.

"Probably bring 'em down next Sunday," Dennis told him. "Let 'em have one more week of summer grass. Pete and I are going to relieve Sparkie and Clyde.

Clyde has one heck of a toothache, says the whole side of his face is swelled up."

One of the men chuckled again. "If it's one thing Clyde can't stand, it's somethin' wrong with his teeth. He'll ride all week with his arm half broke, but he sure can't take a toothache. Never could."

Hank came out. "They said they were low on oats, so I'm sending up enough to last out the week," he told Dennis. "And make sure they leave their cell phone with you."

"Better send along some extra bacon for Pete here," Dennis smiled. "He'll eat my share and more besides."

In late spring or early summer, the fifteen hundred cattle were rounded up from the winter pastures in the valley and driven up the rough terrain to the mountain meadows in the Bighorns to fatten up on one hundred thousand acres of rich summer grass. Two or three men stayed with them, moving them around, doctoring, putting out salt, and making sure the bulls were kept with the cows most in need of their attention. In September, before the snows set in up in the mountains, the cattle were brought back down to feed on harvested hay for the winter. If ever Ryan wanted anything in his life, it was to be up in the mountains all summer with the cattle. But he wasn't asked, and there had never been a boy younger than fifteen to go up with the Saddlebow crew, he knew. Not that there was any rule.

What there was to learn about being a cowboy was not something you picked up on a weekend. Not even in a year. Three years to learn the animals and two to learn the country was about right. It was in the doing, the being with them, that gave you your education, and a summer in the Bighorns was the best way to learn.

Ryan knew a lot—he knew that cattle are best moved early in the day when they're all "mothered up," before the cows and calves become separated from each other in the pastures. He knew the mechanics of putting on a saddle, tightening the cinch, how to ride and how to rope. He knew the etiquette of big sky country—how you never rode another man's horse, you didn't hit another man's horse, you didn't ride in front of anybody. . . . He even knew the weariness that comes from riding up and down hills all day, constantly working your leg muscles. But there was so much more.

Most of what he'd learned, he'd got from Dennis Shay, who never seemed put off by his hanging around. Shay never raised his voice, never insulted. He just watched you do something the wrong way, then rode over and did it right. Showed you a dozen times if that's what it took, and sometimes it did.

"Cow sense," Dennis called it. "There's two kinds of smarts—the kind you get in school, and then there's cow sense, havin' the ability to outthink a cow."

Ryan had enough people-sense to know that he shouldn't ask to go up in the Bighorns with the herd. It was something he had to be invited to do, something he had to earn. And for all the fondness Dennis Shay seemed to feel for him, that Hank seemed to feel, too, they never once suggested that Ryan go, never hinted it might be possible.

Ryan tagged along to the corral to help collect the horses that would go—two each for Dennis and Pete to last out the week. He knew which man favored which—the gray gelding for Dennis, the blue roan for Pete.

Sensing work ahead, the horses galloped around the corral, away from their masters, challenging the men to catch them. A colt wearing a bridle with a long rope attached raced around with the others, stepping on the rope occasionally, which jerked his head and made him slow—one way Hank had of teaching a horse to respond to reins.

"Don't take that one," Dennis said, motioning toward an old white-footed sorrel with a burr-tangled mane. "That's a hard-doin' horse. Let's give her a rest."

After separating them from the others so they could be roped, Ryan watched as Dennis Shay cast the rope, his wrist turning downward when he released it, and the open loop fell over a horse's neck. Each chosen horse flattened its ears at the approach of the cowboy, but once the lariat was around its neck, it stood submissively, prepared for the work ahead. Ryan went about getting the saddles—the rattlesnake-trimmed saddle for Hank—and helped load the last of the week's supplies and the high-protein food the horses would need into the four-by-four pickup that would take the bundles as far as the high corral.

"Thanks, Daddy Longlegs," Pete said when Ryan handed him a filled canteen, and they all watched, amused, while Dennis Shay topped off his horse—took it for a short run to use up that early morning energy and settle it down some. The gray blew clouds of vapor from its nostrils.

By the time the sun was first showing above the barn, the other men left for the hay field, and Dennis and Pete set out on their mounts, rain gear tied to the back of their saddles, the other two horses following closely behind. Ryan sat on the fence of the corral watching them leave. Dennis turned when they reached the old juniper tree where they'd head north, and waved.

The horses broke into a steady trot, feeling the early morning sun beginning to warm their flanks. The pickup was already far ahead, disappearing over the first hill. Ryan jumped down and walked back toward Hank's house. He ached with the wish to be a part of that crew on their way to the Bighorns, listening to the crunch of hoofbeats, the creak of leather, the occasional snort of the horses and the wry comments of the men.

"You closed that gate, didn't you, Ryan?" Mrs. Floyd called, coming to the door.

"Yes, ma'am," he replied, knowing that an open gate in cow country could lead to big trouble.

The sky was turning from gray to blue, and crimson thickets lined the bank of the river, dotted with cottonwoods and aspens. Ryan walked with his head turned toward the two men who were growing smaller and smaller in the distance, and it wasn't until he heard Debbie Floyd say, "You want some breakfast, Lon?" that he realized his father had come over, too.

"Naw, I'll just take a cup of coffee," Lon said, and limped toward the porch. Mrs. Floyd turned back inside to get it, and Ryan and his father watched Dennis and Pete disappear among the trees, heading for the rougher hills ahead.

"Sure wish it was me out there on a horse," Lon Walker said at last. "Useless old bag of bones. Stay here long as I have and you get to be like one of the old horses; they can't shoot you, so they just keep you around."

"Wish I was going, too," said Ryan. "I don't figure they're ever going to ask me."

His dad just snorted. "It's Gil they should be asking. He could make a fine cowboy if only he'd put his mind to it."

Three

Some Sundays, if Dad woke early, he'd make pancakes when everyone had time to eat them. But when Ryan got up the next morning, he didn't smell any cooking, which meant that Dad was sleeping in. Which meant his back was bothering him again.

Ryan had asked his father once if there wasn't any more the doctors could do. And his dad had answered, "There's an operation, but no guarantee it'll make me any better; a fifty-fifty chance it'll make things worse. So I'll just ride it out. Not the way I'd hoped to be spending the rest of my life, but I don't have much say in it."

Freddy was on the trundle bed a few feet away, his mouth open, making little popping sounds as he slept.

He looked somewhat like Dad—brown hair, big chin, heavy eyelids—except that on Freddy, they looked young; on Dad, they looked old.

The house was quiet. Charlene was sleeping in, too, and Gil had already left for his weekend job of pumping gas at Teepee's. Ryan decided to take the mare and ride over, have a doughnut for breakfast.

There was mist all around him, fog obscuring the tops of the cottonwoods; the mountains weren't visible at all. With no cars on the road and no machine sounds coming from the shed, Ryan could hear the river as it trickled over the rocks; he liked that sound. Wished there was a bridge, a real Walker's Crossing, where folks could get to the other side instead of driving way down to Eagle Pass Road.

He met his mother coming from the barn.

"Where you off to?" she asked.

"Riding the bay to Teepee's. Haven't taken her out all week."

"Well, you chop that firewood when you get back," was all she said.

The bay mare tossed her head when she saw Ryan, seemed to know what he was up to. She liked to run but hated the bridle—the bit in her mouth—and he had to work up to it, taking his time. He brushed the snarls out of the reddish-brown back, talking to the animal all the while. The mare turned her head in Ryan's direction, nuzzling her nose up under his arm as though expecting to find a sweet.

"Nothin' sweet about my armpit, I'll tell you that,"

Ryan said affectionately, then got the saddle and blanket down off the wall and adjusted the stirrups.

"Your feet hang any lower, you'd be rakin' ground," Dad had said, amused at the length of the stirrups whenever Ryan rode. From the waist up, Ryan didn't look much different from anyone else, but he had the longest arms and legs of anyone he knew.

He kept the bridle behind him as he approached the horse a second time, rubbing her forehead with his other hand, stroking the black mane, and then expertly slipped the bridle and bit into place and crooned his thank-yous.

"Now aren't you a good girl! Aren't you a pretty one! Want to go for a run?"

The bay swished her black tail and turned expectantly as Ryan opened the door of her stall. How come it was so easy talking to horses and so hard talking to girls? How did Matt do it, didn't even have any sisters? Ryan guessed that when girls thought you were cute, you could say anything at all and it would come out of your mouth sounding cool.

The paint was out in the pasture, but the roan whinnied from the neighboring stall, needing a run as well. Charlene had promised to take him out this weekend, so Ryan let him be. Charlene, in fact, had her eye on the rodeo the following May, working up a little act with some of her girlfriends for the amateur part of the program.

Ryan grinned to himself. Who was she kidding? Charlene wouldn't be satisfied till she'd made rodeo queen, riding around the ring carrying the flag. Well, it could happen. She was getting to be a pretty fair horsewoman.

He led the bay outside, fastened the door behind them, and mounted. Had he followed the road to Teepee's, it would have been seven miles to the state road and five miles beyond that to the junction. But if he went as the crow flew, he could spend a few minutes scrambling over the steep ridge that bordered the valley where the house stood and, like the deer and elk that used the route, be there in less than an hour. The bay mare was strong and surefooted, and made good time.

If there was anything in the world better than this, Ryan thought as he rode, he didn't know what it was. A long-legged cowboy sure had an advantage when it came to mounting a horse. Shay once said that all Ryan had to do was throw one leg over the animal and he was ready to go.

There were no other buildings as far as the eye could see. No smokestacks, no water towers, no billboards. Just miles and miles of rolling hills—some green, some brown, some mottled with gray and gold—rising, falling, ending at last in the sharp, rocky peaks to the west, more distant mountains to the east. These were Ryan's boundaries, and the sky was half his world. He could be content if he never saw San Francisco or New York City, he was sure. As though the mountains were guardians of the valley and all he loved.

Woods, hills, pasture, prairie . . . woods, hills, pasture, prairie. . . . He had heard people say that you could get hypnotized by the rolling surf at the ocean, but he felt he could drift off, dream off, just riding up one hill and down the next, watching the changing sky. Today the clouds had a scalloped look, as though someone had thrown scoopfuls of whipped cream into the air, and they were spreading slowly out with the wind, etched against the blue.

Dennis Shay once told him, "Sure don't need no church out here. Why, every day of my life I'm in the most beautiful church God ever created, the prairie under my feet, the sky above."

T. P. Bates was large for a man, and his place was big for a truck stop. It was hard to miss, day or night. You go by night, you'd see the glow of the neon sign before you could see the long cinder block building. Go by day, and it would be the sign again that you'd see first, highest thing on the land, next to the mountains, of course.

Ryan had left the dogs behind this time. The best thing about Sunday morning—next to riding in on the bay mare—was sitting on a stool at the lunch counter in Teepee's, Aunt Peg telling him he could pick anything he liked from the doughnut safe.

Aunt Peg was Dad's sister, and she'd worked her way up from waitress to manager of the restaurant part of the truck stop in only three years. She and Ryan got along just fine. He never helped himself to a doughnut until she invited him to; then he'd carefully lift the plastic top, studying the chocolate-covered doughnuts, the fried apple fritters, the coconut or the cream-filled cakes, and when he'd made his choice, she'd fix him a cup of hot chocolate with a pyramid of whipped cream on top.

Ryan would sit on that stool in his cowboy boots and hat and see how long he could make it last. She never regarded him as a freak, either. Only thing she ever said to him about his height was, "There's no use feuding with the body you got, 'cause it's the only one you're going to get. You don't make peace early on, you'll be fighting it all your life."

Well, maybe, Ryan had thought. Aunt Peg never had to put herself in size twelve shoes, though.

"Where's your buddy today?" she asked as she wiped the coffeepot. She was on the slender side, with short gray hair and wire-rimmed glasses that she always forgot to clean until Ryan reminded her.

"Can't even make out the color of your eyes, Peg," he'd tell her.

Then she'd laugh and put down the tea towel she carried with her, take off her glasses and say, "Why, I *am* half blind, aren't I?", clean them, and stick them back on again, tucking her hair behind her ears, behind the tiny pearl earrings that she'd worn ever since Ryan could remember. She always dressed in a Western shirt and jeans. The truckers liked her that way.

"Matt?" said Ryan. "I don't know. Sometimes he comes and sometimes he doesn't."

"If I was sure he was coming, I'd save that devil's food doughnut for him, but those always go first."

"Doesn't matter," said Ryan. "He'll live."

T. P. Bates didn't have the best location in the world for his truck stop, but it wasn't the worst, either. It had been there five years before the interstate came along and, as a consequence, sat two miles west of the major thoroughfare. But almost every trucker going from Montana to Mexico had heard of Teepee's, and most of them figured it was worth the detour. Word got around that Teepee's had good food, low prices, and Western-style clothes. There was a mechanic on duty twenty-four hours, and usually somebody around to help at the pumps. Some said they'd make that detour just for Aunt Peg's four-alarm chili, Paul Bunyan burgers, home fries with sausage, and apple-cheese pie.

"You see those two men over by the window?" Aunt Peg told him. "They've been stopping here for three and a half years. Seems like one's always going south 'bout the time the other's heading north, and they get together on their CB radios. Whenever they can, they meet here for a cup of coffee and some pie."

Ryan studied the men. One had a Chicago Bears cap on his head with the bill in front, and one wore a Seahawks cap with the bill facing backward.

"What's unusual," Aunt Peg went on, "is that one of those men is a Republican and one's a Democrat, and they argue over every little thing. Yet they *listen* to each other." She smiled. "For a gal who never went to college, I expect I've got about the best job there is. Folks coming in here from over the whole United States. I keep my ears open, I'm bound to learn a little something."

After he'd finished his doughnut and Matt still hadn't come, Ryan went outside and over to the gas pumps. Gil worked on construction jobs with Richard Sheldon when there were any to be had, but on weekends he worked for T. P. Whenever Ryan came by, he'd work at washing customers' windshields. That always won new friends for Teepee's. He liked climbing up on the big rigs, seeing how far over the windshield his long arm would reach.

"So help me, boy, you got an arm on you could probably do the whole windshield from one side," this morning's customer declared. "Your ma got you on growth hormones or something?"

"No, I'm just naturally tall," Ryan said.

"Play basketball?"

"School hasn't got a team. When I get to high school, maybe."

Gil wasn't saying much this morning. His eyes looked a little puffy, as though he hadn't had much sleep. He still looked good, though, probably the best-looking one in the family, and clearly Mom's favorite. "That boy could charm his way out of a paper bag," she always said, and Dad seemed to feel the same; *used* to think Gil could succeed at almost anything he put his hand to.

That, of course, was before Gil, the summer after

he'd left high school, told the folks he was going over to Gillette to apply for a job in a coal mine, but went off to Denver instead with a buddy to see what work they could pick up there. Sonny, his friend, got a job nights tending bar, and Gil got work in a video store. But Sonny got fired for coming to work late too many times, and Gil didn't much care for his boss, so they were home again in a month.

Strange how different he and his brother were, Ryan thought. Ryan wanted to be a cowboy in the worst way, do just like his dad did once, what Hank Floyd was doing now. Gil didn't care for it much. He did what work he had to on the ranch, but never volunteered.

"I want some kind of job where I don't take orders from anyone but myself," he told Ryan once after Moe had chewed him out for something. "Not going to have any chili-picker telling me what to do." Which was the first time Ryan had realized Moe Morales was Mexican.

"Well, you either take to ranching or you don't," Dennis Shay had told Ryan. "No shame in deciding you'd rather do something else."

Gil never quite decided one way or the other, though. He worked sometimes at Hank's but was often just "too busy" or "too tired" to go over there. He and Sonny talked about going off to Colorado again and starting a rafting company, but nothing came of that, either. There were the construction jobs, Teepee's, none of them anything that seemed permanent. Dad kept urging Gil to settle down, but it never happened. The puzzling part was that Dad really wanted his boys to follow in his footsteps, yet he almost never praised Ryan. Never once told him he was proud of the way he got up early on Saturdays and went to the foreman's house, made himself available to do most anything Hank asked him to. Ryan figured that if Dad ever did pass a compliment his way, it would mean he'd given up on Gil, was turning his attention to Ryan, and that's something he guessed Dad wasn't ready to do. So Ryan continued to wait for his chance, Gil continued to dawdle, and Dad withheld his praise till he could see which way the wind was blowing.

"What time you get in last night?" Ryan asked finally as Gil let a wide yawn take over his face and leaned against one of the pumps.

Gil snapped his jaws together and gave him a weary grin. "You sound just like Ma," he said. He looked like his mother—hair red as a Wyoming sunset. He had wide shoulders, big arms with tattoos on both of them. "Got in early enough to get some sleep before I came here. That suit you?"

"Some car was pulling out when I got home from Matt's Friday night," Ryan told him. "Had its lights off. Someone looking for you?"

"How would I know? What were they driving?"

"I couldn't tell. It was dark. An old maroon two-door, I think. A Dodge, maybe." Ryan thrust his hands in his pockets and waited for the next car to pull up. "Matt keeps talking about government spies coming out here to check up on us. First thing I thought of—if that's who they were." He expected Gil to laugh, but he didn't.

"Any spies hanging around here, they sure aren't going to introduce themselves," Gil told him. "They'll come in disguise—like ordinary truckers, maybe, having an ordinary piece of pie at the counter. And first thing you know they've got your Social Security number, your gun, and finally, your land."

"But *why?*"

"Oh, you'd be surprised," said Gil. "You'd just be surprised."

Four

Ryan hung around Teepee's for another half hour looking at jackets and boots he couldn't afford, and knives and caps he didn't need. Finally, when Matt still hadn't come, he went back out, mounted the bay, which stood droop-headed, reins tied to a fence rail at the end of the parking lot, and started home, passing his mom as she pulled into the parking lot, heading for Teepee's with a batch of sticky buns she'd baked the night before to sell in the truck stop restaurant. She didn't enjoy baking, particularly, but it was one way to bring in extra money, and jobs out here were scarce. She'd had her application in for a year to drive a school bus, but the only thing open so far was substitute driver.

Charlene was supposed to be watching Freddy, but she was reading a magazine.

"Where's Freddy?" Ryan asked, throwing his jacket on a chair.

"I don't know. Outside somewhere. Dad's here."

"Where's Dad, then?"

"I don't *know!*" She glared at him over her magazine. "*Some*where!"

As it turned out, Dad was still in bed, and Freddy was hanging over the fence of the bull pen. It seemed to Ryan sometimes that the Walker family was going off in six different directions; it wasn't the way it used to be when Dad was a cow boss and Mom's voice was a little softer.

"Don't you be falling into that bull pen," he told Freddy. "Why don't you go in the house and watch cartoons or something while I chop the firewood?"

"No cartoons on Sunday," Freddy complained. "I was just going to feed the bull some hay."

"You won't be feeding that bull anything. He gets plenty. You want to feed something, try the cows. We got four of them going to calve in November."

"They're going to have baby cows?"

"Yep. Calves."

"How do you know?"

"'Cause we bred 'em last February."

"What's that mean?"

"Let the bull get to 'em. Then you count the months to see when the calves will be born. Dad breeds ours early so they'll be done calving before the Saddlebow cows begin. We'll sure be busy then."

"Is the bull going to have babies, too?"

Ryan grinned. "No. He'll be the daddy. I'll tell you all about it when you're older. Come on, help me give Midnight and Sergeant a bath."

They used an old horse trough behind the barn. The dogs came when Ryan whistled, but were reluctant about it, and stood shivering, dejected, in the long, half-filled trough, while Ryan applied the shampoo. He and Freddy rubbed and kneaded, and when Ryan gave a second whistle, the dogs leaped out, shook themselves vigorously, happy once again. Then they loped off to see what mischief they might roll around in, Freddy after them.

Ryan collected the wet towels and had just started back when he saw Matt Sheldon coming around the side of the house looking for him, madder than a wet cat.

"What's wrong with *you*?" called Ryan.

"Why'd you go blab about the Red Man?"

"What do you mean? It fell out of my pocket. Ma saw it and asked where it came from. What was I supposed to say?"

"Well, now Mom thinks I chew."

"You and about every other guy around here."

"Your ma tells mine I gave it to you, and I tried to explain how I found it, but she don't believe me. Says I put one foot in hell when I put tobacco in my mouth, and if I like the smell of strong stuff that much, I can clean our outhouse."

Ryan stared. "What . . . ?" He could hardly contain a smile. That sounded like Matt's mother, all right, because Mrs. Sheldon was against every sin there ever was and more she made up herself. "You don't *have* an outhouse," he said.

"That one out back of the barn we use sometimes, smells to high heaven," Matt said. Then he bellowed, "What you smirking for? Your ma doesn't believe you, either. When mine says I got to clean the outhouse, yours says she'll put you to work shoveling out your barn."

Ryan wasn't grinning anymore.

"That's not fair! I didn't have anything to do with that Red Man."

"You took it, didn't you? Wasn't me who stuck it in your pocket."

"You're crazy as a coot!" Ryan hollered.

"Yeah? You're crazier!" Matt yelled back.

A window upstairs slammed open.

Ryan stopped yelling and looked up to see his dad, standing there in his T-shirt.

"Okay, you two guys put your fists up," Mr. Walker thundered.

Ryan and Matt stared.

"Go on! Do like I say!"

Mouths hanging open in surprise, the boys put their fists up tentatively like boxers, still staring up at Lon Walker. Charlene had heard the commotion and came out on the back porch, her hand in a box of Cracker Jack.

"Dukes up!" Ryan's father yelled again at Matt. Matt raised his fists a little higher.

"You boys want to fight on a Sunday morning, wake the dead, you go right ahead. Go on! Fight it out! Lick the livin' daylights out of each other, or I'll come down and do it for you."

Ryan and Matt turned toward each other. In the few years they'd known each other, they'd wrestled, had snowball fights, water fights, pelted each other with hickory nuts, but they'd never had a down-and-out fistfight.

"What are you waitin' for?" Ryan's father yelled again. "What have I got down there—two yella bellies?"

The boys each took a step forward. Ryan made a little jab at Matt's shoulder. Matt, shorter by far, grazed his rib cage. Ryan wasn't sure, but he thought Matt was trying hard not to laugh.

"Quit pussyfootin' around!" Dad shouted. "Do I have to come down there and show you cowards how to fight?"

Who was he angry at? Ryan wondered. Dad with his bum leg and back couldn't fight a chicken. Maybe that was it. Maybe the sight of Dennis and Moe riding off toward the Bighorns yesterday—something he used to do—was more than he could take.

Ryan took another light jab, and this time Matt stumbled dramatically backward. Then he pretended to hit Ryan hard in the stomach, and Ryan crumpled in turn. Finally they each jabbed at the other and, unable to restrain themselves, pretended to knock each other out and sprawled helplessly on the ground.

"Well, if you aren't somethin'!" Dad called in disgust. "You got any more fight left in you, do it with your fists. I don't want to hear any more yellin' on a Sunday when I'm trying to get a little sleep."

The window closed again, and Charlene came down off the porch. She stood over them a moment, still eating her Cracker Jack, then shrugged and went back in the house.

Ryan and Matt lay there, fighting off laughter, and finally Matt said, "Man! Who rang *his* bell?"

"I don't know," Ryan answered. "He sure hasn't been himself lately. Feels useless. Says he's 'put out to pasture.'"

They thought about that awhile.

"I hope I can ride till I'm eighty years old," said Ryan. "Dennis Shay says one of his biggest fears is being hung up in a stirrup, or having a horse fall with him and not being found till it's too late. I think I'd rather die on a horse, though, than any other way I can think of."

"You know how my dad thinks he'll die?" asked Matt.

"How?"

"A shoot-out."

"What?" Ryan rolled over on his side.

"Like at Ruby Ridge or something. He says the way things are going, the government's going to take the guns away from every law-abiding man in the West, but he'll never give his up, and if they come after him, they'll have to come shooting."

"Oh, heck. The government doesn't want your guns. Not unless you're planning a war or something."

"You don't know *what* the government will do, Ryan. You ought to talk to Dad sometime. *He'll* tell you."

Ryan lay back, one arm across his forehead, and watched the clouds, like enormous parachutes, spread out across the sky. He was beginning to feel kind of stupid, as though all sorts of things had been happening lately and he wasn't paying attention.

"Well," he said, "maybe I will."

Seventh grade was definitely harder than sixth. Ryan had been a B student, but now he had to work harder to keep up. In sixth, he'd noticed, it had seemed easier to guess the answer—what the teacher wanted you to say, anyway. Now Mr. Phillips seemed more interested in what the students thought. No one had ever shown much interest in what Ryan thought before.

The bus ride was the same, because middle and elementary were in the same building. He still had to get up at six each morning, wait till Charlene finished fixing her hair in the bathroom so she could drive him the four miles to the school bus stop before she drove on to high school.

In social studies on Monday, Barry Dubinsky handed Ryan a list of all the Native American tribes that had lived west of the Mississippi. For much of the first semester, the class would be studying the western states—their history, geology, products, laws . . . Matt and some of the other guys were researching gold and uranium deposits, and Sheila Harrison was working on law and justice.

"How'd you find this?" Ryan asked Barry, glad to have it. The guy *did* have dark eyes and hair.

"Work!" said Barry. "Actually, I found it over the weekend on the Internet."

He *must* be a Jew, Ryan was thinking, to have a computer. Weren't all Jews supposed to be rich?

"Well, thanks," he said, tucking the printout in his bag.

"If you're doing treaties, what do you want me to do?" asked Barry. He scanned the teacher's outline. "We've still got language, family life, religion . . ."

"I don't know. Whatever you want," said Ryan.

"I'll start on language," Barry said. "Tomorrow we can pool what we've got so far."

"I'll hit the library during study period," Ryan told him. He watched Barry go on down the hall. He seemed nice enough. Maybe he wasn't Jewish.

At lunchtime, Sheila stood just ahead of Ryan and Matt in the cafeteria. Ryan couldn't help wishing she were in his and Barry's research group. She, too, had dark eyes and hair—curly hair—and her eyes did all the smiling. At least it seemed that way to Ryan, because every time she looked at them, she seemed to be smiling even when her lips weren't.

They saw her hesitate over a Sloppy Joe.

"Boogers on a bun," Matt murmured over her shoulder.

She turned. "That is so gross!" she exclaimed, but her eyes were dancing. She took the grilled cheese instead.

Encouraged, Ryan added, "The Indians ate dog."

"Yeah? Well, we eat lamb," said Sheila.

"Puppies!" Ryan told her.

"My, aren't you full of interesting information!" she said.

"Come on, Sheila," urged a girl up ahead.

"Yeah, hurry it up, Sheila," Matt teased. "You're holding up the line."

It was the first time she'd really spoken to Ryan, and he was pleased. But Matt was so smooth; Ryan didn't know how he did it. Ryan would never in a million years think of telling a girl she was eating boogers. But Sheila knew how to take a joke. He wondered if he knew any jokes that would make her laugh, and tried one out on the guys when he slid his tray onto their table.

"Why do Mexicans eat refried beans?" he asked. Gil had told it to him the day before.

Matt grinned. "Why?"

"Because they couldn't get it right the first time."

The guys hooted—Matt and Kevin Butler and Scott Mullins.

Kevin lowered his voice, his grin spreading even wider across his broad face. "How do you know when a Jew hits puberty?"

The guys were laughing already.

"I don't know," said Scott. "How?"

"They take the diaper off his bottom and put it on his head."

Ryan didn't get it.

"You know," Matt explained, "that little cap Jews wear on their heads to synagogue. What's it called?"

"A yarmulke," said Kevin. "Geez, don't you guys know anything?"

"I never met any Jews," said Ryan.

"You've met Barry," said Scott. "That nose is the giveaway."

"And the jingle in the pocket," Kevin added. "If he's got a big nose, dark hair, and a fat wallet, he's Jewish."

Ryan worked hard in the library during study period. If he had work left over and had to stay in the library after school, he missed the bus and had to call for someone to pick him up, an hour's drive round-trip. If Dad's leg was bothering him, Mom had to come, and she'd announced she'd picked him up at school for the last time. If he didn't get his library work done in time to take the bus, he was out of luck.

"Either you aren't trying hard enough, or they give too darn much homework," she'd said. "What those teachers don't realize is that kids up here *work* for their food. They don't sit around waiting till a truck brings it to the table."

Freddy had tried to imagine it. "A dump truck?" he'd asked.

The family had laughed.

"What she means is, there's not so many steps in between," Dad had explained. "Around here we raise our own beef, butcher it, freeze it, and cook it. East of the Mississippi they get their meat from the store."

When the final bell rang at the end of the day, Ryan had found at least some of what he needed for his report. The record of treaties broken, however, made them seem more like declarations of war:

The Bannock (l850s): the whites came bringing small-pox, reducing the tribe from 2000 to 50;

The Shoshone: the whites showed little interest in their land until gold was discovered in the Great Basin; broken treaties followed;

Nez Percé (l855): a treaty promised them a reservation, but when gold was discovered in l860, their land was reduced by three fourths;

The Arapaho (Nov. 29, l864): Sand Creek, Colorado: U.S. troops killed many who were camped under the flag and protection of the U.S. government;

The Crow: stripped of l30 million acres granted in l851;

The Sioux: broken promises led to the massacre at Wounded Knee;

The Blackfoot (l870): war breaks out after a massacre by white militia; Grant orders the reservation boundary moved farther north than was originally agreed. . . .

What kind of a country was this? Ryan wondered. Maybe everything the Sheldons believed was true. Look what happened at Waco. Look at Ruby Ridge.

Maybe the government could do bad things to people right here in the heart of Wyoming.

He hoped that the incident of the Red Man tobacco had been forgotten, but no such luck. Mother was making biscuits when he got home, and he could smell the sausage gravy she'd pour over them at supper. He was feeling in an especially good mood, when she had to ruin it all: "That barn's still waiting to be shoveled out, Ryan."

"I did it last time. It's Gil's turn," he protested.

"You know why you're doin' it twice in a row, don't pretend you don't," she said, pressing the biscuit cutter down on the thick dough.

"Okay! I'll do it!" Ryan said irritably. "But I didn't have any taste of that tobacco. It's Gil you should be taking out after."

"This isn't about Gil, it's about you."

"Well, he sure seems to get off easy these days. He's never around."

"He'll be around when the calving starts, don't you worry," said Mother, using her forearm to push back the wisps of red hair that hung down over her face, leaving a smudge of flour on her forehead. "Gil's got a dozen plans all traveling through his mind at one time. Said he got some sort of promotion in that outfit of Richard Sheldon's. Brigade commander or something, I think he said."

So what else was new? Whatever kind of outfit that was, Gil would have to be commander. Ryan went into the other room and sprawled on the couch beside

47

Freddy, who was watching a *Batman* rerun. He was still there twenty minutes later when his mother yelled at him from the doorway:

"Ryan, you got lead in your boots, or what?"

He pulled himself up off the couch, realizing he'd actually fallen asleep.

"You'll never set the world on fire, that's for sure," Mother said as he went past her out the back door. "No siree, you'll sure never light up the sky."

Out in the barn, Ryan took the shovel and began. He hated it when she talked that way. Hated the way she took a piece of your present to cover your future. As if the fact that he was a half hour late getting to his work in the barn meant he'd never amount to any-thing—do anything worth noticing. She just had this way of shooting off her mouth before she thought things through. Maybe that was because she'd never made it to seventh grade. Mom had only gone as far as fifth, she'd told him. Lived so far out in the desert, she was taught by her Aunt Mary what little she knew, and she figured that was enough. Dad had got himself through high school, though—then six months of electrical engineering before he figured it was ranch life for him.

They seemed smart enough in most things, Ryan mused, as he tossed the manure and straw out the open door at the back and onto the manure pile. The main difference he could see between folks who didn't have a lot of school and the folks who did—his teachers, for example—was that the college people always figured there was more to learn, and the people with the least education—his parents, anyway—seemed to think that if they didn't know it already, it wasn't worth learning.

When the stalls had been scraped clean of muck, Ryan took the pitchfork to the stack of clean straw in one corner and began tossing it into the stalls. Two kittens watched sleepily from the top of the stack, undecided about taking a nap or watching the show. One forkful . . . two . . . three . . .

On the fourth thrust, however, his fork thunked against something.

"Not another broody hen's nest," he thought, climbing halfway up the stack to check it out.

It was not a nest full of eggs, but a long cardboard box tied with twine.

Ryan looked at the box for several minutes before he decided to untie the twine. There was no name on it, after all, and it was in their barn.

The lid came off and Ryan found himself looking down on a folded pup tent, poles, stakes, rope, maps, and . . . there at the bottom . . . an automatic rifle.

Five

Ryan was sure the box was there for Gil, but he decided not to tell his father. Not now, anyway. Because Dad had called him a yellow belly, perhaps? That, combined with the fact that if he said anything against Gil, he was just making it extra hard on himself. He retied the twine and put the box back where he found it, then went to find his brother.

The pickup was parked in the clearing beside Mom's old Chevy, and the horse Gil favored—the paint—was missing, so Ryan knew Gil was out somewhere on the Saddlebow.

"You know where Gil is?" he called to his father, who was going into the machine shed, hobbling on his bad leg.

"He's out checking fences," Lon Walker said. "Try the south pasture."

Ryan went back to the barn and saddled up the bay mare. The horse trotted briskly, large nostrils inhaling the scent of autumn. A yellow storm cloud passed overhead, its bottom edge smooth, the top edge ruffled. The bay nickered low in her throat at the distant rumble of thunder.

Another month—weeks, even—and there would be snow frosting the sagebrush, the river coated with ice. Now was the time for repairs—missing shingles, loose wire on the fencing, a broken window, a rusty hinge. . . . Except for calving time when every hand was needed, Gil's work around the ranch was sporadic at best, and didn't make up for the jobs Lon Walker could no longer do. But Ryan's father had worked so faithfully for the Saddlebow for so many years that he had been given this home for the rest of his life.

Ryan saw the horse before he saw his brother. The irregular patch of white on her left flank made her stand out in the dull brown of the pasture. The paint had a habit of shifting sideways when she was impatient to be off, and she danced when she saw Ryan riding toward them, Midnight and Sergeant at his side.

"Hi, P. S.," Gil called. It was a joke between them; it stood for "Pipsqueak," and Ryan smiled. He and Gil had never been really close—there was an eight-year difference in age, for one thing. But Gil had been patient enough to teach him to ride, to fish, to swim, to drive, even, though Ryan couldn't get a license till he was fourteen, and then it was just to drive back and forth to school. They had entirely different builds; unlike Ryan, Gil was stocky, muscular, and topped off at five foot ten.

"What's doin'?" he asked.

Ryan rode up and stopped, allowing the horses to nuzzle each other. The dogs gave Gil a cursory sniff and went racing off to investigate a more intriguing smell.

"Found something in the barn just now I figure's yours," Ryan said.

Gil didn't even look up. He was pulling a huge clump of sagebrush off the fence—a clump as big as a refrigerator. "Yeah? What's that?"

"Box with some camping stuff in it. And a gun. Looks like an automatic to me."

"Yeah, it's mine. Goin' to the camp with my buddies next weekend, get some practice in." Gil picked up the stretcher tool and worked to make the wire tight, the fence secure.

"Sheldon's group?" asked Ryan.

"Yeah."

"What is it? Like the National Guard?" he asked.

Gil grunted. "Ha! We may have to guard you against the Guard someday. No, it's just public service. Public service for the private citizen, you might say."

"So how come you hid the stuff?"

"I didn't hide it. The boys probably dropped it off one night when I was gone. I told 'em to put it in the barn if I wasn't here. You wouldn't want them to set it right out where Freddy could find it, would you?"

"I guess not," said Ryan, relieved. "You going to tell the folks, though?"

"Sure. I'll get around to it."

He got around to it at dinner that evening. Charlene had made the cheerleading team at school and obviously expected to be the center of attention, but Gil grabbed the spotlight.

"I'm going off this weekend with Sheldon's men. We're going to do some drills, start getting ourselves in shape. Won't be home till Sunday night." He winked at Mom. "You make any of those sticky buns, save some for me. Okay?"

Dad looked at him over the green beans. "You check this out with T. P.? He find someone to cover for you at the pumps?"

"Yeah. Says to be careful, not get my ass blowed off or nothing."

"What you getting yourself in shape for? This one of those war games things?" Dad questioned.

"It's not a game," Gil told him, unsmiling now. "Someday you just may call on us for something when the Guard's not around to do it."

Dad seemed somewhat amused, Ryan thought, as he reached for the gravy and poured it over his biscuits. "And what might that be?"

"Keep the state free, protect your home, help you keep your job. . . ."

"Sounds good, except I don't have no job right now to keep. Unless you count shuffling about the Saddlebow, and they could pay an old broken-down horse to do that," Dad said.

"Well, it just might be that somewhere around here there's a job you *could* do with your bad back and leg, but if there is, it's gone to some immigrant who hasn't been around long enough to salute the flag. And before you know it, that immigrant's kids'll have our house and land, 'cause we can't afford to pay taxes on it any longer."

"It's not us payin' the taxes, Gil. The Saddlebow takes care of us."

"But if it *was* our house . . . ," Gil argued.

"How do you figure all that?" asked Mother.

"Let's say some of those Orientals come over here, and they like the look of this country—all this space. So a couple of 'em buy up the best property around and fix it up. Maybe even buy Teepee's for more money than T. P. ever saw before."

"So what's wrong with that?" asked Ryan.

"What's wrong," said Gil, "is that the value of land goes way up. The Japs get a couple more families to move over, build some fine houses, and Saddlebow's value doubles but so does its taxes."

"So, Saddlebow could sell out and get rich!" said Charlene, holding a piece of biscuit on her fork, studying it a moment, then popping it into her mouth.

Caught up suddenly in the argument, Lon Walker jerked around and looked at his daughter. "Yeah, little girl, and where would *we* go?" he asked.

Gil took over. "What if a man wants to stay right where he is, where he's a God-given right to be, but the property taxes get so high he can't afford his own place any longer? That happens, he's up a creek, 'cause the only way he'll see the value of his land is to sell it."

Dad grunted. "Heck, I'm up a creek if the Saddlebow sells out, 'cause we're sure not goin' to get a rent-free house anywhere else, I can tell you."

"Especially if you don't have a job—if the Japs have a corner on that, too," said Gil. "And supposing some little slant-eye comes along and takes a fancy to Charlene."

"I'm not marrying any Jap," said Charlene hotly.

"Yeah," Gil went on, "but there's Japs and then there's Japs. There are the yellow-skinned with slanty eyes kind you *know* are Japs, and then there's the half-breeds you can't quite tell by looking. Except, you marry a half-breed, and the genes are there, and your kids could all end up pure yellow." He laughed. "You get a mixed-blood of *another* kind, your kids could be something a *heck* of a lot different. That's what happens when you mix the races. You don't see horses and cows mixing. Sometimes the animals show more sense than we do."

"*I* seen horses and cows together!" declared Freddy.

Everyone laughed.

"That's not the kind of together I'm talking about," said Gil.

"It's all there in the Bible," said Mother, "the way the races scattered after the flood and divided the way God intended."

This isn't making any sense, Ryan thought. Mom was talking about races of people, but horses and cows weren't even the same animal. "You crossbreed different kinds of cows to get the best," he said, still trying to figure it out. "Dennis cross-breeds Hereford, Angus, and Shorthorn, and says they give more milk."

"Yeah, but you crossbreed people, and you just might get the worst, too," said Gil. "You're mixing in the bad with the good. You got to stick with purebreds from the right races."

"What do you mean?" asked Ryan.

"There's twelve countries to choose from," said Gil with an air of authority. "And here's the way to remember them: Start out with the U.S. and Great Britain, and then you think of two things that a dog will do—DIG and SNIFF with an H and an S left over: United States, Great Britain, then **D**enmark, **I**taly, **G**ermany, **S**weden, **N**orway, **I**celand, **F**inland, **F**rance, plus Holland and Spain."

"Are you talking about races or countries?" Charlene asked.

"You stick with those countries, you're okay," Gil told her. "Won't have to worry about mongrel children."

Ryan couldn't tell if his father was amused or concerned. "Now, Gil, where'd you pick all this up?" he asked, frowning a little.

"From people who've made a study of it, know a lot more than we do," said Gil.

How did life get to be so complicated? Ryan wondered. He'd never learned any of this in school.

"Dig and sniff!" laughed Freddy, trying to be part of the conversation as he lined up his peas on the side of his plate and ate them one by one.

"We study it over at Sheldon's," Gil went on. "Meet out in his barn. He's got it all right there in a book."

"But what you getting into? What kind of a group is this, anyway?" his father asked.

"The Mountain Patriots' Association. We got us a dozen people and we're recruiting every day. You just might be needing us sometime."

That part appealed to Ryan—somebody needing him. "Who all can join?" he asked.

"You have to be eighteen, but we've got a junior cadet corps. You can always come to meetings. Matt does."

But Dad wasn't convinced. "Don't you fellas go off on any crack-brained scheme you haven't thought over some," he warned. "Sheldon's okay, but he's pretty intense, you ever get to talkin' to him."

"Better patriot than most of us'll ever be," Gil observed.

And Mother said, "I'm proud of you, Gil. Always knew you had it in you to join somethin' important."

Dennis and Pete wouldn't be back with the herd till Sunday, so when Saturday came, Ryan sat on the porch swing with his father and watched Gil leave in the pickup. The rest of the cowboys were haying, Ryan knew. It was late in the year for hay, but everything seemed to be running behind. Spring had arrived late, and now summer was hanging on. Haying was about his least favorite job on the ranch—the scratchy hay pricking his arms; the hay dust in his nostrils, his throat; mosquitoes adding their little bit of misery. He decided to skip.

Gil was dressed in his camouflage suit and army boots. The camping equipment and food were in the back of the truck, but he had kept the gun in the cardboard box, Ryan noticed. Didn't show it to their father. Hadn't told him about it, either, and that made Ryan wonder. He especially wondered because he remembered now that the night he'd seen a car leaving Walker's Crossing with its headlights off was the night he'd gotten in trouble over that Red Man tobacco. And the night Ma chewed him out for that, he'd remembered hearing Gil and his boom box down in the basement. So Gil had been home when the men came by, and still they hadn't come to the door.

"He had a gun in that box," Ryan said at last, feeling he had to, as the pickup went under the crossbeam at the end of the lane and turned at last onto the road.

His father didn't speak for a moment. Just kept pushing his feet against the wood floor of the porch, the swing making a creaking sound each time it came forward. "Well, you can't hardly go on maneuvers without a gun," he said finally. And then after another minute, "What kind was it?"

"Assault rifle. Looked to me like a Uzi. Mr. Sheldon has one. Matt showed it to me once."

"They only shoot blanks in practice, I'd guess," Dad said, but Ryan saw that he was nervously drumming his fingers on the arm of the swing.

Ryan didn't know why he said what he did next, probably because his dad seemed to take the gun too lightly. But he added, "Well, I saw a car coming out of our driveway last week with its headlights off, and I'll bet those were the guys who put that gun in our barn. I found it there with all the camouflage stuff. Why do you suppose they're sneaking around with their lights off?"

He also hadn't counted on what happened next. His father turned suddenly and give his face a slap.

"Dad!" he said, astonished.

His father seemed equally confused, staring first at Ryan and then down at his own hand.

"Well, maybe you had that comin', boy," he said, his face reddening as he settled back uncomfortably against the swing. "What you tryin' to do, sitting here firing one thing at me after another about Gil? You got something to say against your brother, say it all at once, don't be givin' it out a piece at a time."

"Fine!" said Ryan, getting up and storming over toward the door. "Fine with me. You don't care what Gil does, neither do I."

Man, this really ticked him off. It wasn't the first time he'd felt that Mom and Dad should have stopped having kids after Charlene. He'd been an afterthought, he decided. And then, eight years later, when Freddy came along, well . . . poor Freddy.

He banged around inside the house until he was sure he was going to get a crack across the mouth, and decided he'd better head for Teepee's. The sooner he got there, the better. That was one place he knew he was welcome.

"Can you drive me to Teepee's?" he asked Charlene.

"You want to go now?" she said, standing in front of the living room mirror applying mascara to her lashes. Charlene was always good for a drive to Teepee's.

"Yeah," Ryan told her.

They climbed in the Chevy and started down the drive, the sky threatening, a deep purple-gray looming up over the horizon. Ryan took off his hat when he was in the car, but his head almost touched the ceiling, anyway. He had to keep his knees pointed out at the sides to fit in the front seat.

"For Pete's sake, Ryan, get your knee away from the gear stick," Charlene scolded. "Everytime I take you anywhere, you just spread out over the whole front seat."

Wordlessly, Ryan shifted his feet and pulled his knees in.

"What was Dad bellowing about out on the porch?" she asked.

"Standing up for Gil, as usual," said Ryan. "You breathe a word against Gil around here, you're in for it."

"Firstborn," Charlene said knowingly. "I read all about it in my psychology book. Dad's worried about him, I think. Parents expect the most of their firstborn and want him to be all the things they aren't, and Gil doesn't have a clue."

"Then they must not expect anything at all from us," Ryan said dryly.

"Look at it this way: *We* get to do anything we want!" Charlene said. "Frankly, I hope it takes me a long, long time to decide what I'm going to do, because I want to have all the fun I can first." And when Ryan didn't answer, she said, "What about you?"

He shrugged. "I'd be happy just doing what Hank and Dennis do—live right here on the Saddlebow. Get to be cow boss some day, have my own place. . . ."

"I'd rather be a trick rider and travel around to all the rodeos. Get to see the country," his sister told him.

"Takes a lot of practice, Charlene."

"I know. I'm taking the roan out this afternoon. A bunch of us girls are working up a little act for the amateur show next May."

"Don't get yourself killed, now," Ryan said, and grinned.

At Teepee's, Charlene headed for the clothing section, Ryan toward the restaurant. "I'll be going back in about an hour. You stay longer than that, you've got to get yourself home," she said. "Okay?"

"Okay," he agreed.

It appeared to be a busy day at the truck stop, seven big rigs parked in the open space behind the sprawling cinder block building. Ryan had been all set to go inside and get his free doughnut when T. P. called to him.

"Hey, Ryan!"

61

T. P. Bates was a broad-shouldered man with a big belly. He liked his steak and he liked his beer, but most of all he liked having truckers from all over the country stop by. He always asked the men to sign a register by the door, telling the state they were from or where their cargo was going, and if it was a state that hadn't been listed yet, another little flag went up around the big mirror that greeted you as soon as you walked in Teepee's restaurant.

There were forty-five flags now. The only states Teepee didn't have yet were Alaska, Hawaii, New Hampshire, Georgia, and Alabama. He'd about given up on Hawaii, but Aunt Peg had convinced him that even a driver who had been born in Hawaii could qualify, so T. P. kept a lookout for a driver from out in the Pacific.

"Listen, Ryan," he said. "The fella who was supposed to take Gil's place today didn't show, and I'm busier'n a one-armed cowboy. How 'bout you helping out at the pumps? You need a ride home later, I'll drive you."

"Sure!" Ryan hoped he was going to get paid, but he didn't say anything.

"You lame or somethin'?" T. P. asked as Ryan started across the concrete. "You're walking funny."

"I am?" Come to think of it, those boots did hurt. His toes jammed hard against the ends.

"My feet are gettin' too big for my boots, is all," he said.

"Tell you what. Stick with me all day—take time off for a sandwich at noon—and you can pick your own boots, all but the expensive ones there in the window. Deal?"

Ryan could hardly believe it. "Deal!" he said. Man, oh man! Did he ever like this!

Most of the people who stopped at Teepee's pumped their own gas, but some had trouble with the nozzle or couldn't read the directions, or didn't know where to pay, and everybody wanted his windshield cleaned. Must have been that every trucker within a hundred miles of Teepee's came by that day, it seemed to Ryan—every driver who wanted the antifreeze checked, every citizen needing a new battery before winter set in, every resident wanting a new set of snow tires. The sky reminded folks of the months to come, but except for a few isolated raindrops, the storm passed them by.

Ryan worked straight through till three, then took a break only because Aunt Peg made him.

"Ryan, you get yourself in here and have a sandwich with me," she yelled from the restaurant doorway. And when he came inside, she said, "Why don't I make us both a grilled cheese and bacon and some fries? Oughta plug up the arteries good, but I figure we'll work it off." It was sort of a joke between them, because no matter how much they ate of anything, she and Ryan, neither seemed to put on any weight. Fat just didn't stick.

"I'll wash my hands," Ryan said, and when he came back to a booth, she had a double malted waiting for him as well.

"Whew!" Aunt Peg sat down at the table and kicked off her shoes. "The other girls can run the counter for a while; I got a bunion the size of Rhode Island driving me wild." She reached down to massage her foot, then took a big drink of her own malted. "So where's Gil off to today, so important he couldn't come in?"

"It's some group he's joined over at the Sheldons'. Like a club, I guess. Only they protect people," he said, and took a big bite of grilled cheese, the bacon crunching against the roof of his mouth. His right knee bobbed up and down with pleasure.

"A club that protects people! What's he going to, the Policemen's Ball?" she asked dryly.

"No. The Mountain Patriots' Association. Something like that."

"Sure must be a lot of protection out there," said Aunt Peg. "Haven't heard of Gil's bunch, but that word 'patriot' sure gets around." She chewed without smiling.

Ryan took a good long drink of the malted, savoring it on his tongue. Aunt Peg made them so thick and chocolatey, the straw stuck straight up in the glass; didn't even lean. "He says if there's ever a time the National Guard can't defend us, that's when the Mountain Patriots will take over. And don't be surprised, he says, if they end up having to guard us against the Guard."

"How nice," said Aunt Peg, without enthusiasm. "Somebody in here from Texas last week was passing out leaflets about the Southern Aryan Federation. Now I'd expect something like that from Texas, maybe, or Montana or Idaho, but not here in Wyoming."

"What does that mean—Aryan?"

"White," she answered, raising her eyes suddenly to look at him, then picking up a piece of bacon on her plate. "Not only *white,* but the right *kind* of white."

"Yeah, Gil said there are twelve nations, and if you marry a purebred from any one of those countries, you'll never have mongrel children."

"Mongrel children?" Aunt Peg's voice suddenly spread across the restaurant, and she checked herself. "Now just what does Gil mean by that? We're all mongrels, Ryan. We've got all sorts of blood running through our veins, and what does it matter?" Then, "Sorry. I didn't mean to pick on you. So what are those twelve purebred nations, did he say?"

Ryan tried to remember the acronym: "Great Britain, the United States . . ."

"The United States?" she asked incredulously. "The United *States?* Well, you better go looking for an authentic Native American, then, when you get around to marrying, Ryan, because everyone else who came after don't count, us Walkers included."

T. P. told him he could quit about seven, he had another man coming to take the night shift, and Ryan was glad.

"You choose those boots yet?" T. P. smiled.

Ryan nodded. "I'll take the ones with the cactus

design on the sides, the camel-colored ones over there next to the clock. Size twelve."

T. P. smiled. "Sort of figured you might like those. Problem is, do we have your size? Let me check. . . ."

That was always the way. Ryan had never bought a jacket yet whose sleeves were long enough. Same with jeans. You had to hunt to find thirty-six-inch inseams, and even those were beginning to look too short.

T. P. stuck his head out of the stockroom. "What width you take? Narrow? Medium?"

"Narrow," said Ryan, waiting.

T. P. grinned. "You're in luck. Got two pairs, in narrow and wide, and one of 'em's yours."

He brought them out, and Ryan walked around a little in them, reveling in the sharp sound of the heels on the wood floor, admiring the shape of the toe.

"Guy your age came in last week with his dad and bought a pair something like these," T. P. said. "Dubinsky. You know him?"

"Yeah. We're working on a project together at school," Ryan said.

"They sure seem to take to Wyoming. The dad works for the government, I think," T. P. said.

Ryan looked up. "Like the CIA or something?"

T. P. looked at him curiously. "I don't know. I didn't ask."

Six

Sunday morning, Ryan rode the bay mare over to Hank's before the sun was full up. He loved the honking of wild geese at dawn, and the "Whooo" of a Wilson's snipe at dusk. Mostly, he loved everything there was about Wyoming—the Floyds' place in particular—and was waiting on the steps when Debbie Floyd turned on the light in her kitchen.

He was feeling guilty about not showing up the day before when the men were haying, and wanted to prove he was dependable.

"I swear, Ryan, you might just as well move in," she said jovially, sticking her head out the door. She was on the short side, somewhat plump, and her blond hair was naturally curly, a tangle around her face. She was also as freckled as a speckled egg.

"I don't need breakfast or anything," he told her. "I just wanted to be here when the herd gets in."

"Well, you're going to come in here and eat with me whether you want to or not," she said, laughing now. "Hank decided to ride up early this morning and help bring the herd down. I need some company for breakfast."

Ryan didn't have to be asked twice. He followed her inside and set the table; he'd been there so often, he knew right where things were.

"They'll probably get back around noon," Debbie said as she threw some slices of bacon in the skillet and adjusted the flame. She pointed to the cell phone there on the table. "Wonderful invention," she added. "I can remember when the only way you knew the herd was back was when you saw them over the rise of the hill. Now I can have the food on the table about the time the men reach the porch. Things sure do change." She glanced over at him. "So how you doing, Ryan? How's school?"

He shrugged. "Okay, I guess. Not my favorite place to be, exactly."

"Or mine," she said. "It wasn't that I didn't do well in school. . . ." She frowned a little, as though trying to figure it out. "I just didn't like being shut up inside those four walls. Maybe if we'd had classes out on the prairie I would have liked it better, but I'm a cowgirl through and through. Can't imagine doing anything else with my life."

"Me either," said Ryan. "I could live right here, never step outside Wyoming, and I'd be happy."

He hoped she'd say, *Well, why don't you?* Or, *I'll ask Hank to take you on.* But she said, "That's the way Hank feels. He ever has to go to town, it's real hard on him. He can take a herd of cattle, he says, but he sure can't take a herd of people."

They both laughed.

"I'm sorry I didn't make it over yesterday. I was helping out at Teepee's," Ryan said, fudging the truth.

"Hey, listen. It's not as though you're on the payroll," Debbie told him.

"Well . . ." Ryan hesitated. "I'd sure like to be." Debbie only smiled, so he asked, "When do you think they'll take the herd up next summer?"

"If the snow in the mountains is slow to melt like it was this year, it could be July, I suppose." She turned the bacon, then stood looking out the window, one hand on her hip, her suede vest worn and spotted above her jeans. "Jiggs and the others finished up with the haying yesterday, but I told them to come back around noon today, we'd have us a good meal."

Breakfast tasted great, especially because Debbie put a piece of apple pie on the table, seeing as how she hadn't made biscuits. "Go ahead, eat it," she said. "I'm going to make a couple more this morning—have 'em waiting when the guys get in."

"You want me to milk your dairy cows?" he asked.

"I already saw to that. Milking's my 'thinking time.'" She grinned. "It's when I get everything straight in my mind. But you can clean out those water troughs, anything else that needs doing. Don't think Moe's got

69

to it yet. You know the work almost as well as I do."
She turned on the radio, then got out the flour and
lard.

By now the sun was up, and Ryan let it warm his
face and neck. There wasn't anything about Hank's
place he didn't like. He liked the look of the land, the
lowing of the dairy cows, the ones Debbie kept for her
cream and butter. Liked the smell of the hay, the manure, even. The sound of the old Fordson tractor. He
liked the summer greens and yellows, the winter
browns and golds, ice on the pond. He liked the way
Debbie Floyd talked to her cats, Hank talked to his
horse, the way Hank and Debbie talked to each other.
Their children, all grown, had left the ranch, and
when Debbie said she was glad to have Ryan around,
he believed her.

Most mornings Hank drove his pickup into the
horse pasture in the hills above the house. When he
blew the horn, the ranch horses would come for their
breakfast of oats. But he must have left that for Moe
today in order to leave early, Ryan decided, because
the horses had gathered and watched Ryan expectantly. Most were plain browns and bays with no particular markings.

"Okay, you guys, breakfast!" Ryan called, going
into the barn for their oats, pleased he got to it before
Moe did.

After that he brushed the horses who would allow
it, took the hose and cleaned the water troughs,

stacked some firewood, then practiced roping fence posts, knowing that roping a moving target from a moving horse was something entirely different. Finally, about eleven, he went back to where he had tied the bay, mounted, and rode out to the hill in the direction he expected the herd to come.

When he reached the crest, he stopped and let the horse graze while he sat erect in the saddle, his eyes on the horizon, the bluest blue there could possibly be. If he didn't look behind him at the camp house, he was seeing the land the way it was when the Shoshone and Mountain Crow people roamed Wyoming. If he shut out the wire fencing, he could be an Arapaho brave, waiting for a scouting party to return. That was what he liked about the West, this piece of it, anyway: There wasn't anything between him and all that had gone before—no cement sidewalks, no telephone poles, no billboards or malls or parking meters—just him and the same land the first Americans had walked on. It was almost as though, if he remained quiet enough, he could hear their whispers.

High above, so far away it made no sound, a plane was making a vapor trail. Below him, a tumbleweed half the size of a horse went skittering along the valley floor.

Ryan had been waiting fifteen minutes or so when his ears picked up a sound . . . a man's voice, perhaps? . . . a faraway call, and then the lowing of cattle. Back down by the house, Ryan could see Jiggs and the other men, gathering for lunch.

The herd.

He tightened the reins, bringing the bay's head up, and waited as one small, dark figure—then another and another—appeared over the crest of the next hill. The calls became more distinct:

"Hey, there! Move it—move it!"

"Yee haw! Get on up there!"

The calls were punctuated by the slap of a man's gloved hand against his leather chaps as he zigzagged back and forth to keep the herd heading in the right direction, and accompanied by the constant complaining of the cattle. Back down by the house, Ryan could see Jiggs and the other men, gathering for lunch.

Ryan watched to see whether the cattle were being herded toward the north or the south holding lot, then went racing back down to open the heavy, tightly strung gates, something he had not been able to do until this year. Even then, it took every bit of muscle he could muster. He was pleased when he saw Dennis Shay, riding point, wave his hat in thanks before the herd, sensing familiar territory, came hurrying wild-eyed after the lead cow, eager for the meal and the water that waited for them.

"Get the south gate, too," Dennis yelled.

Ryan was already headed in that direction, and was disappointed when Moe suddenly appeared, galloping by, and beat him to it. The five dogs who had gone up with the herd in June stuck to their job, barking and circling, knowing, perhaps, that tonight they would sleep on Hank's porch after a good meal.

Hank, on his buckskin gelding, was riding at the

side to keep the line from bulging, and far behind, Pete was riding flank, separating the herd, moving the second half toward the south lot. Ryan circled around and fell in beside Hank.

"I fed your horses and cleaned the troughs," Ryan told him.

"Much appreciated," Hank said. "You seen Debbie?"

"Yeah. We had breakfast together."

"Good. You'll stay for lunch?"

"Sure."

Before anything else, however, the arriving cattle and horses had to be tended to. When the horses were placed in the pasture, they rolled and grazed, glad to be rid of the hot and heavy saddles. Later the cattle would be separated—some shipped off to feedlots where they would be fattened on grain, some to remain until they reached market size, and some of the finer specimens to stay on as brood cows or heifers, replenishing the stock.

Dennis and Pete were dirty, dust filling the creases of their necks, the folds over their eyelids. It was caked in their fingernails, the lines of their palms. Nevertheless there was banter and laughter as Jiggs and Clyde and Sparkie drove up from the other end of the Saddlebow, and they all washed up at the pump in the yard, making generous use of the pile of towels Debbie had put out for them.

"Debbie, hon, I'm only goin' to get the first layer off, so's I won't be eatin' dust, but the rest'll have to wait till bath time," said Pete. The men laughed.

"Heck, Pete, we were eatin' dust all summer. What you got to complain about?" said Clyde.

"Took Clyde and me a week just to get at the dirt under our fingernails," said Sparkie.

"Hey, Clyde! How is your toothache?" Moe called.

The potbellied man with the thinning blond hair hooked one finger in the side of his mouth and pulled, revealing a dark empty space near the back, and the men laughed again.

"You got that twenty you owe me, Sparkie?" asked Jiggs. "I been waitin' since Christmas."

"You waited this long, you can wait till next Christmas, and I'll pay you back with interest," Sparkie said, and the men hooted.

Debbie looked at Dennis Shay. "So how did this last week go?"

"We had a pretty good blow one of those days, but it was a good spell. Got every head accounted for," he told her. "Lost a horse, though. He stepped in a gopher hole and broke a leg. We had to shoot it."

Debbie's face fell. "Not that chestnut gelding with the white on its nose. . . ."

"It was a flea-bitten gray, but a good workhorse. Was real sorry to lose it," Dennis said.

It was fun to sit at the large table and listen to the talk and banter of the men. Now that the bulk of the work was over—the driving of cattle, the haying for those left behind—now that they all had a good bed waiting for them, they were in fine spirits, weary as they were. They were talking about what would happen during the slack months of October to March.

74

"Well, once the calvin' begins, it sure won't be no slack time," Jiggs said. "I'll be back around then, you give me a whistle."

"I like the ridin', but I sure don't take much to calvin'," said Pete. "Told my wife if I wanted to deliver babies, I'd have worked in a hospital."

The men chuckled.

"You better believe it," said Dennis. "It's those heifers that'll make you sweat. You get those first-time mothers . . . heck, some of 'em don't even know a baby from a bucket. They'll spill right out there in the field, then walk off and leave it."

Ryan drank in the voices of the cattlemen, savoring their inflections, their faces, the jokes that passed between them, their ribbing and joshing. Funny how silent they always were at breakfast, the day stretching out before them, and how talkative they got once their work was over and they could let down a little.

"Last year, with fifteen hundred cattle all calving at once, I didn't know if I was ever goin' to sleep," said Hank, resting his elbows on the table. "I left one heifer to see about another, and when I come back, the calf had been dropped, but I couldn't find it for love or money. I tell you, my feathers fell right then. Figured it had been dragged off by who knows what, but then I hear this bawl, and out of the bushes it comes. Its mother wouldn't touch it."

Jiggs shook his head. "Sometimes you just gotta say to those heifers, 'It's a baby, Stupid!'"

The whole kitchen shook with laughter.

And then Moe Morales said, "We needing any help

next summer, I have a nephew. Big, strong boy. Sixteen years."

Ryan felt his heart sink in dismay, his temples throb, and he glanced down the table at Hank. Surely Hank wouldn't say yes, not with Ryan sitting right here, practically one of the crew!

"Where's the boy now?" asked Dennis.

"He's with my sister down in Tucson, but he could live with me, my wife," Moe said.

"Well, we'll see how it goes," Hank said simply, and put another loaf of bread on the table.

Seven

Unless there was a blizzard or something, Teepee's always had a party on Halloween. It went from three in the afternoon, when they gave out free cider and doughnuts, till midnight, when the coffee, too, was free. Longtime truckers who knew they'd be around that part of the state on Halloween would often come in with masks over their faces, and together T. P. Bates and Aunt Peg and some of the other employees would try to guess who they were. If there wasn't snow, high school students always gathered at Teepee's on Halloween to dance out in the parking lot, and a good number of students from the middle school showed up, too. Almost everyone came in costume.

Meanwhile, Mr. Phillips was expecting the students' preliminary reports. "By Halloween," he said, "you should know the history of the western United States better than you ever did before, and by the time the unit ends, you should know your particular area of study like the back of your hand."

"How you doing on the treaties?" Barry asked Ryan after class one day as they were heading to gym. He was usually the one who started conversations between them. Ryan was more inclined to keep his distance. He was polite, though.

"I found a lot that we broke, but I can't find any we kept completely," Ryan told him. Then he added, "We were sort of rotten to them, you know?"

"Yeah, that's what my dad says."

Ryan glanced at him. "He works for the government, doesn't he?"

"State government. Game and Fish Department. Why?"

It wasn't the CIA, then. "Just wondered. Where'd you live before?"

"Oregon. But Dad likes Wyoming best. Used to spend his vacations here. We might even buy a house. Mom misses Oregon, though—her friends at church."

Church? Ryan wondered. *Not synagogue?* "What church?" he asked.

"Catholic."

"Dubinsky's *Catholic?*"

Barry looked over at him and laughed. "It's Polish, that's all I know."

Well, what do you know! Ryan thought. He *still* hadn't met a Jew.

At lunchtime, he and Matt had just reached for their bowls of chili when a voice behind them said, "Looks like dog food."

They turned to find Sheila laughing at them.

"Okay," Matt said, grinning. "I deserved that."

Matt sure knew how to talk to girls, Ryan was thinking. It wasn't fair. Matt hadn't been around girls at all—he'd been home-schooled till sixth grade—yet he talked as easily as though he'd known her all his life, while Ryan, who had lived around Charlene for twelve years, was tongue-tied. Of course, when Matt had started sixth grade, he wasn't easy with girls, either. It was only when a couple of them started whispering about him—flirting with him—that he seemed to lose his shyness. Maybe it could be like that for Ryan, too. When Sheila talked to Matt, though, they were more or less at eye level. When she talked to Ryan, she had to tip her head way back. What girl wanted to go around with a pain in the neck?

After she got her tray, however, Sheila followed Ryan and Matt over to their table where the other guys were waiting, and sat right between them, smiling all the while. *That's what made it easy,* Ryan thought as he opened his milk carton. Her smile. If girls just knew how important that was to a guy. When a girl smiled at you—like Sheila did, anyway—it said, "Come on over and talk to me. I won't embarrass you." So many girls put on that sultry, pouty look, as though it would kill them to be a little friendlier. If a guy made the first move, Ryan figured, a girl could at least help him out.

The guys were talking about the coming party at Teepee's.

"Remember last year, when two of the truckers came as Dracula, and pretended to fight it out?" said Kevin.

"Your aunt Peg is craziest of all," said Scott Mullins, turning to Ryan. "Everybody remembers the time she dressed up like T. P. Bates—got his wife to loan her his T-shirt, put a pillow under it, and had a cigar hanging out the side of her mouth." They all laughed.

"You ever go to Teepee's on Halloween?" Matt asked Sheila.

"I think my sisters went once," she said.

Scott grinned at her. "You have sisters? Cousins?"

"Why? You desperate?" Sheila joked.

"No. Just gregarious."

"Greg . . . what?"

"I've got a lot of friends," Scott said.

"That's good," said Sheila.

Ryan watched enviously as Sheila asked Matt if she could trade her dill pickle for a package of his crackers. A girl just didn't trade food off her plate unless she liked you, did she? Man, it looked so easy.

Scott said to Sheila, "Did you know you were eating with two cadets?"

"Yeah?" said Sheila. "Who?"

"Matt and Kevin."

Sheila turned and studied them. "What kind of cadets?"

"Mountain Patriots' Association," Kevin told her. "Impressed?"

"Am I supposed to salute or something?"

"A couple bows will do," Matt said, and laughed.

Ryan was curious, and as he left the cafeteria with Matt, he said, "What was that about cadets? You and Kevin?"

"We joined the MPA."

"Your dad's club?"

"It's not a club. It's more like a militia."

Ryan tried not to appear envious. "What do you do? Put on a uniform and march around?"

"Come over sometime and see," Matt told him.

Gil didn't get home till Monday evening—had stopped off to visit some of his buddies on the way back, he said—and Mother made him take his boots and socks to the basement. The dogs followed him down to feast on the wild scents he brought with him.

"Whew, Gil! You guys get to stinkin' like that, you could guard the whole country just by airing your armpits!" she exclaimed.

"Slept in a tent the first night, in a foxhole the second," he told the family. "I guess if you get tired enough, you can almost sleep standing up."

At dinner, after a shower and a change of clothes, he was full of stories about his marksmanship—how he got the bull's-eye six tries out of ten. How they took an oath to defend each other, their homes and families, against enemies both foreign and domestic.

"Who's the leader of this outfit? Who's got the responsibility?" asked Dad.

"Dick Sheldon. Bet he could run for governor if he wanted—*make* it, too—except the country's too corrupt," Gil said.

Maybe he should join, Ryan thought. At least he'd have something to talk about if he ever found himself sitting beside Sheila again. He wished now he had been included when Scott told her about Matt and Kevin.

"We've teamed up with a Federation over in Sandpoint," Gil was telling his parents, pulling a folded newsletter from his pocket and placing it on the table. "They're going to announce it in their next edition."

"Well, now, that's something!" Mother said. "This organization of Sheldon's is going places, looks like."

But Lon said, "I can't quite figure Dick Sheldon out. Was he in the service?"

"Vietnam. Man, he has seen it all. He knows the government inside and out!" Gil told them.

"So if he knows enough to run for governor, what's he doing way up here in the Bighorn Basin, hardly anybody knows where he lives?" Dad insisted.

Gil pointed to the newsletter again. "Sometimes you have to get away from corruption in order to see it clearly, he says. These people over in Sandpoint—they know what they're talking about. Read the newsletter. You'll see!"

When he'd finished eating and the discussion had turned to other things, Ryan took the newsletter into the living room and lay down on the couch to read it. He liked the symbol on the front. It showed a man with a rifle slung over his shoulder. He was holding a little baby in the crook of his arm and had his other arm around his wife. Behind them, the American flag.

The Patriot Leader, it said at the top, and below that, *Myles A. Reddick, Editor.*

At the very bottom of the page, in a box, it said, *Food for Thought: We stand for what America once was, and must be again.*

Are you ready and willing to go all the way? asked the lead article by Mr. Reddick. *Which of the following still connects you to a corrupt Zionist-controlled government? Driver's license? Social Security? Birth certificate? Hunting license?*

If you can't give them up all at once, the article said, then do it one at a time. A journey of a thousand miles begins with a single step. Keep going till you're off the umbilical. Off the grid. If you need more proof that the army of the New World Order plans to take over these United States and make slaves of your sons and daughters, consider these recent reports by reliable sources. . . . And a list followed:

By the year 2006, every newborn baby in America will have a microchip installed in the palm of his left hand, so he will be subject to government surveillance.

Markings on the backs of stop signs are coded direc-tions to guide invading United Nations forces.

Surveillance cameras have been found hidden on the tops of street light posts in Portland.

Black helicopters sighted over Montana are preparing to take over the National Guard.

A salt mine near Detroit is being readied for U.S. males who resist a takeover.

And on the back page it said, *Stay prepared! When Armageddon comes, remember your three B's: Beans, Bibles, and Bayonets.*

There was a cold rain Halloween morning, to the huge disappointment of both Ryan and Charlene, be-cause it could be snow by evening. It often was. Trees that were golden with autumn at dawn could be winter-frosted by night. But by midafternoon, the rain had stopped. The sun came out now and then, and though the clouds were surly looking, blown by the late Octo-ber wind, and the temperature fell, the wind died down by evening.

Charlene and some of her girlfriends were going to Teepee's as a salad. Charlene was the tomato. Ryan and Matt, however, went as a toilet bowl and brush. Matt had worked up a cardboard toilet seat to fit around his middle, with a lever at the side. Every time anyone pushed the lever, Matt made a whooshing sound with his lips.

Ryan dressed himself in black. On his head, he

wore a huge Styrofoam rectangle into which he had laboriously poked the bristles of two old brooms he'd dismantled. The headgear made him even taller, seven feet, at least. He and Matt had been working on their costumes since September, and though they had to be worn over down vests and hooded parkas, anyone could tell what they were supposed to be.

Mrs. Sheldon had said she'd drive the boys, and came by the house early to bring Mother a jar of her blackberry jam.

"Now *that* will be good on biscuits," Doris Walker said, holding the door open wide as Matt and his mother came in. "Can't you sit down a minute? Ryan's just putting on his shoes." She nodded toward the couch where Ryan was tying his sneakers.

Martha Sheldon was even leaner than her husband, with cheekbones that poked out on either side, and long, straight hair hanging halfway down her back. She wore jeans and a leather jacket that looked as though it belonged to Matt's dad.

Lon Walker edged Freddy off his lap and straightened his pant leg. "You see the costumes our boys have cooked up?" he asked, grinning.

Martha Sheldon gave a reluctant smile. "Halloween's not something we celebrate at our house, but Matt was like to have a fit if I didn't let him go. We don't do any of this devil worship, but I guess his walking around like a toilet bowl won't do much harm."

Doris Walker took the boys' side. "I can't see how

Halloween's going to hurt 'em one way or the other. If all they do is parade around Teepee's parking lot, I can think of a whole lot worse they could be doing."

"I'm going, too!" Freddy said excitedly. "Dad's going to take me over later."

"I'll drive the boys home," Dad told Mrs. Sheldon. "Save you the trouble. How are things at your place these days?"

Ryan was impatient to be off, but he didn't want to appear rude. He and Matt wiggled their eyebrows at each other.

"It's been a hard year," Matt's mother answered. "Dick's still making payments on that backhoe. Figured we'd have it paid off by now in construction jobs, but not a whole lot's going on."

Lon Walker agreed. "Things are slow all over. I'm thinking of selling one of our cows, ease things for us a bit." He rubbed one side of his face. "Gil says he's been over to your place a lot lately. This group of Richard's . . ."

Mrs. Sheldon nodded. "Dick's made him commander of the A brigade. You should be proud of the way Gil's taken to this. Dick holds his meetings in the barn so's not to keep the kids up. Some weeks they get ten, fifteen people out there."

"This just a local group, or you got ties to something national?" Lon asked.

Mrs. Sheldon waved the question away. "We're all over. Go by different names, but you'll find folks like us in every state of the Union. It's all based on the

Bible, you know. People just don't realize how close we are to the breaking down of society, just like the Bible predicts. The millennium is here! It's time! Dick was never more serious about anything in his life."

"Time to what?" asked Mother, looking puzzled.

Ryan shifted restlessly, but Matt was listening to his mom now.

"'Come out from them and be separate, and touch not the unclean thing,' the Bible says," Mrs. Sheldon told them. "And I don't think it means a good woman with her hand in the bread dough or a man who makes an honest living by the sweat of his brow. It's us who live up here in the mountain states trying to protect our land and our children and our way of life who are trying to be separate, and it's men like Dick and Gil who will do the protecting. That's what it's all about."

"Protect you from what?" asked Dad, ignoring Freddy, who was tugging at him, trying to get him up and going.

"Famine, disease, pestilence, invasion. . . . It's all there in Revelation. You can read it yourself. But when the city folks flock out here begging us to feed them, when it's every man for himself, the Mountain Patriots will be ready."

"Mom," said Matt finally, tapping his watch.

She smiled sheepishly. "Just get me started . . . !" she said. "I got the twins asleep out there in the back seat, and these boys want to get to Teepee's." She stood up. "Nice talking to you both. You come by sometime."

"Good night, Martha," said Mother. "We'll get together soon."

Maybe it was the roar of the big semis as they
pulled into the lot; the whistles and calls, one trucker
to the next; the laughter as a trucker climbed down
from his rig in a gorilla mask—sometimes even a whole
costume he'd acquired just for the occasion. The frosty
air, the outdoor lights, the music, the crowd . . . It was
simply the place to be on Halloween night, cold as it
was. Ryan felt like an Eskimo beneath his costume in
his down jacket and mittens and hood.

Everyone seemed to be there—even Mr. Phillips,
the new teacher, dressed as a penguin. The girls' gym
teacher came as Queen of Hearts. Ryan didn't see
Barry, but Scott and Kevin were there, and they and
Ryan and Matt all trolled the parking lot, looking for
Sheila. They saw a group of kids gathering at the far
end, and found that Sheila and a girlfriend had come
as Siamese twins and were trying to walk without
falling down, to the laughter of their friends.

It was a perfect night. The huge orange moon
seemed like the bright pupil in the dark black eye of
the sky. T. P. ran out of doughnuts around nine-thirty,
and started giving out cookies and candy bars instead.
Ran out of cider and gave out pop. Truckers on the
move still wanted their soup-beans and corn bread,
their biscuits and gravy or chicken-fried steak, so
Aunt Peg and the waitresses were busier than ever. But
every so often she'd come to the door in her Popeye

getup and make the rounds of the crowd, playfully poking a clown in the belly or trying on a fireman's hat.

One of T. P.'s married sons drove up with a couple of horses and a hay wagon, and the costumed revelers, fat in their padded clothes, climbed aboard for a ride around the huge parking lot. On every fence post around the property, a jack-o'-lantern beamed. Did people in other states have as much fun as they were having here? Ryan wondered when some of the kids from school started dancing, and he watched as Matt tried to dance with Sheila and her Siamese partner, ending in a twisted jumble of arms and legs.

It was about ten, just when the crowd was largest, that Ryan heard the low thudding of horses' hooves against the ground, and looked up to see what he thought at first were costumed ghosts riding bareback across the field behind Teepee's. Then he realized they were six men on horseback, wrapped in sheets with hoods down over their faces. The horses, too, had blankets covering their flanks.

Ryan's mind whirled as he tried to think what they were supposed to be exactly. Warlocks? One of them was carrying a large pole, and Ryan decided maybe they were Knights of the Round Table.

The riders galloped around and around in a circle as the crowd, hushed now, drew back, and finally the man with the pole tossed it down in the center of their circle and threw a match on it, setting it instantly ablaze. Ryan saw that it wasn't a pole at all; it was a cross wrapped in strips of burlap—cloth evidently soaked in kerosene, for it was immediately engulfed in flames. *The KKK*.

"Oh, my god!" he heard Aunt Peg say from the doorway of the restaurant.

Ryan stared at the men who were circling now, their eyes, deep within the dark round cutouts in the hoods, the only parts of their anatomy, other than their hands, that were visible.

The men began to chant, and Ryan tried to make out the words. At first he thought they were praying, because it sounded like "Jesus Christ! Jesus Christ!" It took a few seconds to realize that what they were really saying was, "Keep us white! Keep us white!"

And then, as the stunned crowd parted to let them pass, the horsemen charged back out of the parking lot the way they had come.

Ryan looked after them and, as the horses galloped off, their blankets flying, he saw that the very last horse had a large irregular patch of white on its left flank.

Eight

The silence after the hoofbeats had died away was almost as frightening as the riders themselves. The music was still playing, of course, piped out from the restaurant, but the quiet among the spectators, the way they froze in their tracks, like antelope in the beam of a searchlight, was so unnatural that people could only stare at each other.

"God help us," said T. P. Bates.

"Not in Wyoming!" a woman was heard to say.

And then Freddy's voice from somewhere in the crowd: "What were they supposed to be, Dad? Ghosts?"

"Klan," said someone.

"They were probably just playin' around, it bein' Halloween," a man offered.

The Ku Klux Klan. Gil had joined that? Ryan wondered. All he knew about the Klan was that it was some outfit down south that used to dress up in sheets and scare the blacks. Hung some of them, too. What was the KKK doing up here? Hardly any blacks here at all!

"Well, *that* was dumb!" he heard Sheila say.

"Who were they? Who were those men?" People's voices filled up the silence again, but the music had cut off.

"You get a look at any of them?"

"What's the cross supposed to mean? Why a *cross,* for heaven's sake?"

"They don't burn it, they 'light' it," said somebody else. "I had a son-in-law used to be in the Klan. Not as bad as you think."

"So who were they after? This state's already whiter'n Wonder bread!"

"I figure it's just a warning. They know we're white. Just keep it that way, is what those boys were saying."

"How you know they were boys? How you know they weren't some grown men in those sheets? Should have better sense than do a fool thing like that!" shot back T. P. "Sure didn't ride like boys. Rode like men. Cowards, is what they are."

"Better watch it, T. P. They'll be after you next," someone joked.

T. P.'s voice came over the loudspeaker: "Okay, now that we've had a little no-count rabble, which sure won't win any prize from me, let me tell you, let's start the judging for the best costume," he said jovially. "Where the heck are my judges? Sam . . . Billy . . . get on up here . . ."

People began to smile again and congregate over by the entrance to Teepee's, but somehow it just wasn't the same. A lot of folks were leaving. Sheila went inside the restaurant to call her dad.

Ryan wandered dazedly about the parking lot for a few minutes, wondering how a night that had been going so right could have suddenly gone so wrong. Finally he said, "Listen, Matt, I think I'll go on home with Dad. You want a ride?"

"No, I'll go with Kevin," Matt told him.

Ryan took off the Styrofoam headgear and threw it away. Then, without saying good night to anyone, he climbed into the passenger seat of the pickup, banged the door, and was there when his dad came over with Freddy.

"Dang idiots," Mr. Walker said. "T. P.'s mad, and I don't blame him."

"Those ghosts were scary!" Freddy said, grinning nonetheless. He crawled over Ryan, settling in between him and his father.

Still, Ryan didn't answer.

"I suppose those clowns thought it was funny, riding up like that, but it sure upset a lot of people," Mr. Walker continued.

Ryan stubbornly settled himself against the back of the seat, his face a mask, jaw clenched. He sure wasn't going to stick his neck out this time and get a crack across the mouth. He couldn't believe that only he recognized Gil's horse. It seemed his father was giving him every opportunity to accuse his brother, just so he could lash out at him. No way he'd let that happen again.

Once home, he got out of the truck before it even stopped, and stomped on up to the house. "Where's Gil?" he asked.

"I don't know. I expect he was at Teepee's," Mother said.

"Yeah, he was there, all right," Ryan muttered.

"Well, if you already knew, why'd you ask?" Mother snapped back.

Ryan didn't answer. He went right through the house to the back door and took a flashlight out to the barn. The bay and the roan were standing sleepily in their stalls, heads down, but the paint was missing.

It was the next morning when tempers exploded. Ryan had meant to be over at Hank's early—be anywhere but home—but he overslept. Freddy was watching cartoons in the living room, Dad was finishing his coffee, and Ryan and Charlene were eating leftover corn bread and cereal. Charlene was still spouting off about what had happened, and Ryan let her do the talking. Better her than him. She didn't know Gil had been one of the riders, evidently.

"One of the best nights we have to look forward to, and a bunch of nuts ride up and ruin it!" she said. "I was ready to party! John and Patty and Eleanor and I were going to get up this line dancing—all across the parking lot—and T. P. promised to put on our CD. . . ." Here she broke into tears. "I could just kill whoever did that!"

"Now Charlene, you don't have to talk about killin'," said Dad as Gil came into the kitchen in his jeans and socks, the yellow string of a Bull Durham tobacco pouch dangling from a breast pocket. He picked up the carton of orange juice and poured himself a glass.

"Who's she gonna kill?" he asked sleepily, scratching the back of his neck.

"The idiots who showed up in sheets last night and ruined a good party," said Charlene. "Anybody who'd ride around with a hood over his face is a stinking coward."

"Well, maybe you just oughta ask yourself why they did it!" Gil said. "Maybe there's something a little more important to be thinking about than dancing across a parking lot."

"What guys in sheets have to say doesn't interest me in the least," Charlene told him. "We don't need any night riders in this state."

"That's probably what Mississippi and Alabama thought once before the blacks started getting out of hand. That's probably what New York thought before the Jews took over, and California before the Mexicans and fags moved in."

"Gil, watch your mouth," Mother said, nodding toward Freddy in the next room.

Ryan steadfastly said nothing. Absolutely nothing. He stared down at the Wheat Chex in his bowl and let the words swirl around him.

"What you going to do, girl, if you fall in love with a guy and find out his great-grandfather was a coffee-colored nigger?" Gil asked his sister.

"Gil!" yelled Dad.

"Who's talking about marrying, for crying out loud? All I wanted to do last night was laugh and have fun," said Charlene.

"Yeah? Well, then, what are you going to do when you can't get the job you want because the company's got to hire Mexicans first before it can hire whites? What if you go to get your hair cut and it's a homosexual doing the cutting?"

"I don't care who cuts my hair! What difference does it make?" Charlene asked in exasperation. "Why are you guys so worried about homosexuals? You just laugh if you see a rattlesnake or something, but somebody tell you there's a gay on the loose, you get your guns out."

"You know what?" said Gil, his voice rising. "You know what? America is right at the place it was back when we belonged to England, and a small group of men took it upon themselves to say, 'Enough.' Now I don't believe in the Ku Klux Klan exactly, but I'll bet those fellas last night weren't in any way, shape, or form any kind of members."

"Well, they sure weren't the Welcome Wagon," said Dad.

"What it was, in my opinion, was just a wake-up call," Gil said.

And his mother added, "Maybe you ought to listen to what he says, Charlene."

"A wake-up call to go around hating people?" Charlene asked.

"We don't hate nobody!" Mrs. Walker declared, turning potatoes over in the frying pan and hitting the spatula on the edge for emphasis. "It's just a natural thing to want to do for your own kind. Birds of a feather flock together. You ever see two different-colored birds in the same nest? If a man doesn't want to protect his family, keep it special, what kind of man is that?"

"Yeah," said Gil. "They set aside eleven million acres for the spotted owl so it can keep the species going, and when white men want to do the same—just keep a little corner of America pure—why, they holler something terrible."

Ryan mostly listened. He'd been on Charlene's side to start with, but every once in a while Gil would say something that seemed to make sense, and then he'd wonder, was he wrong? All he really knew was that he was confused and angry, because he could see that life was going to be extra tough for him, starting now.

Freddy wandered in from the other room and took up a piece of half-eaten cinnamon toast he'd left on the table earlier.

"Why's everybody yelling?" he asked.

"We're having a discussion, is all," said Dad.

Charlene snorted. "Gil sticks up for those cowards in sheets, there's nothing to discuss."

"Those ghosts we saw last night?" asked Freddy enthusiastically. "That was the best part!"

"Well, maybe they were thinking ahead about some of the problems we've got in this country, but they sure went about it wrong," said Dad.

Ryan finished his breakfast without saying a word, then went out to saddle the bay and rode to Hank's. Most of the men were out in the north lot repairing a pipeline, so he helped out around the house—brought in more firewood, put up a storm window, fixed a loose rain spout—almost anything Debbie Floyd asked him to do.

"You're a good worker, Ryan," she told him. "Most of these young fellas want to dress like a cowboy, their legs hanging down off the sides of a horse, but they don't want to do any of the dirty work."

She looked over at him and smiled, and Ryan smiled back, but for most of the day he worked silently, brooding about things he couldn't control. And when he rode home later, the sky had the cold, dark look of winter, the clouds broiling and twisting as though announcing a visitor uninvited.

Nine

The Walkers' cows were due to begin calving in November, four months before the fifteen hundred expectant cattle on the Saddlebow gave birth in March. Even in November, however, snow could be so deep that Ryan's father could scarcely make it to the barn. But there was no appreciable snow yet, only the feel of it in the air.

It wasn't snow, however, and it wasn't calving that was on everyone's lips at school on Monday, but rather what had happened at Teepee's over the weekend. Not everyone agreed about what it meant.

"I don't know why everyone's so upset," said Kevin. "T. P. said come in costume, and that's what they did. If they were supposed to look like the Ku

Klux Klan, they put on a good show. So what? It was Halloween!"

"Just raising a little ruckus, that's all," said Scott.

In the library, Ryan said to Barry, "What'd you think of what happened at Teepee's?"

"I don't know," said Barry. "I wasn't there."

"You heard about it?"

"Yeah. Dad says it was probably just a bunch of guys acting up."

"Maybe so," said Ryan.

Final reports were coming due in history, and Ryan was so full up with Native Americans, he didn't think he ever wanted to hear about the Sioux or the Arapaho again.

"Why don't we get together over the weekend and finish up?" Barry suggested. "Want to come to my place Friday night—stay over?"

Ryan might have—he was certainly curious—but he knew he might be needed at home. "I'd better not," he said. "We've got four cows due to calve, and Dad'll need us if there's a problem."

"What could you do?"

"Depends," Ryan said. "If nothing else, all the other chores while Mom and Dad tend to the cows. Why don't you come and stay with us?"

So Barry came to school with his things stuffed in his backpack, to ride home on the bus with Ryan after school.

"He's going to sleep at your place?" Matt asked.

"He's Polish, not Jewish," Ryan said.

Matt thought that over. "Poland's not one of the twelve countries, you know."

"So? We're just doing homework together, we're not getting married," Ryan told him.

Freddy had agreed to give up his place in the trundle bed and sleep on the day bed near the kitchen, and seemed glad to have a visitor when the boys got home from school. Charlene had picked them up this time at the school bus stop, and all three came in together.

"Mom, this is Barry," Ryan said.

Mrs. Walker smiled. "Help yourself to the raisin bars there on the table, Barry, before my boys eat 'em all," she said. "Made 'em this morning. Hope you like stew, because I cook everything in one pot when the cows are calving, let folks fend for themselves."

"I like stew," said Barry. And after dropping their things upstairs, he and Ryan went outside.

"I always wanted to live on a ranch," Barry confided once they were out back. "I hope we buy one."

"Well, we're only a piece of the Saddlebow," Ryan told him. "We've only got a few head of cattle, three horses . . ."

"What's your dad do? Is he a cowboy?"

"He used to be till he got hurt. Now he helps with the hay when he can, cleans out irrigation ditches, repairs machines—stuff like that. You ever ride a horse?"

"Some."

"We could saddle up the bay and the roan. Gil doesn't like anyone to ride the paint except him. The bay's mostly mine, and the roan's Charlene's now."

Barry helped saddle the horses, and moved easily about them, Ryan noticed. He rode okay, not as naturally as Ryan, but sure enough, and he didn't freak out when the horses made their way down the steep riverbank and he and Ryan had to lean back almost against the animals' rumps to keep from falling forward.

In time, Ryan was thinking, Barry might make a better cowboy than he would. Dad always said the shorter fellas made better ropers and wranglers because their center of gravity was lower. "They're more one with the horse," he'd said.

It was probably true, but Dad never realized how much that hurt. Didn't realize, maybe, that this was the only life Ryan saw for himself, the only thing he wanted.

The horses picked their way carefully across the shallow part of the river, then climbed up the steep bank on the other side to the far meadow. The roan seemed to know that this was the place he could cut loose, for his legs began to dance when he reached the top, and he blew a cloud of vapor into the cold air. Barry whooped.

"Keep the reins tight," Ryan called. "Don't lose control of your horse. Stop her if you have to."

Barry managed to slow the roan to a comfortable trot, and the boys rode side by side. Ryan pointed out a hawk—two hawks—circling the sky.

"You swim here in the summer?" Barry asked.

"Yeah. And fish for trout. Gil and Dad do, anyway. Gives Dad something to do since he hurt his back."

"Man!" Barry kept saying as they rode along together. "Man! When we get our place, I hope I can have a horse. If I were you I wouldn't do anything else but come out here and ride."

Ryan grinned. "If you lived on the Saddlebow you would. We all have to help out at calving and branding time. In May we have to round up all the calves and separate them from their mothers—treat 'em for pink-eye, maybe. We have to brand 'em, inoculate 'em, de-horn 'em, and, if they're males, castrate 'em."

"Ow!" said Barry, wincing. "Not all at once!"

"Yeah. It's all over in about two minutes. The men rope a calf by the hind legs, drag it to the fire, and wrestle it to the ground, and then they brand it on its side and over the nose. Somebody else inoculates it. The males are castrated, and any calf showing horns has them cut out. They come through okay, though— go scampering and bawling back to their mothers. Takes 'em about six days to recover."

"I wouldn't like that part of a roundup," said Barry.

"I don't, either, except for the roping part. I'd like to get really good at that," Ryan said.

When they got back to the barn, they saw Ryan's mother coming out of the house.

"Well, I was right on target," she said. "One cow's back in the barn—got all the signs of birthing—but that heifer's gone way out by the east fence and she's pushing. Awful small, too, so I'm worried. Go help yourselves to the stew. There's corn bread warming in the oven."

Charlene was already getting things ready when

they went inside. The boys washed up at the sink, then turned toward the table, where a tall stack of soup bowls leaned precariously to one side. There was a cluster of spoons and the pan of corn bread.

Ryan's father picked up a bowl with one hand, the soup ladle with the other. "Say when, Barry," he instructed, hands poised above the stew pot. He put in one cupful, then another, and paused.

"I'll start with that," Barry said. "Thanks."

"Eat up. It's like to be a rough night," Dad said.

Ryan grinned across the table at Barry. "I told you we'd be busy. A lot different from Oregon, huh?"

"You're from Oregon, Barry?" Charlene asked. "How come you're out here?"

"Dad always wanted to live in Wyoming."

"Yeah? What's his line of work?" asked Dad.

"Biologist," said Barry.

"A *biologist?*" Dad said, and gave a little laugh. "And he's out here mixing with us cowhands?"

"He teach school or something?" asked Charlene.

"No. He's a wildlife biologist. It's outdoor work mostly. He just does a lot of different stuff," Barry said.

Ryan wished they'd quit asking questions. It seemed rude. What did it matter what Barry's father did?

Dad changed the subject. "How many you got in your family?"

"Just me and my folks."

"No big brother to pin your ears back?" Dad joked.

Barry returned the grin. "Nope. Enough guys at school willing to do that."

When the table was cleared after supper, Ryan and Barry spread out their papers and began pooling their research so they could each write up a full report. They'd worked only a half hour or so when Mrs. Walker stuck her head through the back door.

"Lon?" she yelled. "You'd better get your jacket on. The heifer's in trouble."

"What's wrong?" Barry whispered to Ryan.

"Having trouble pushing her baby out," Ryan said. "Want to go watch?"

"Sure!"

"Gil's in the barn with the one, but it's the heifer I'm worried about. Take your pick," Mother told them. "It gets messy."

Ryan and Barry put on their jackets and waited till Dad pulled on rubber boots. Then they followed him to the pasture.

"I got the 'come-along.'" Ryan heard his mother's voice from somewhere in the darkness.

"The what?" asked Barry, and for the second time Ryan was pleased to explain.

"It's the winch that we use to help pull a calf from its mother when she's really having trouble."

They followed the circle of yellow light from Dad's lantern, soon joined by the light from Mom's. It was a three- or four-minute walk to the place in the east pasture where the heifer had chosen to calve. She was a dark brown animal with a long white stripe on her nose, and she lay on her side in exhaustion, her head halfway off the ground. Every so often she huffed a little and lifted her head some more. All that was visible from the opening in her body was a whitish sac, like the membrane over an eye.

"Where are the legs?" Barry asked, bending down to see.

"In the sac."

They waited while Mother attached a strong metal chain around the end of the sac, which ruptured suddenly, spilling fluid.

"There, poor dear," Mother crooned to the cow.

When the chains were reattached, this time to the calf's legs, Ryan's father braced the winch with one foot and slowly began to crank the handle. The cow gave a low moan.

Mother's hands, with rubber gloves now, were guiding, reaching, pulling, stretching, and finally, finally, with a sucking sound, a calf was born, and Mother sank back onto the ground, panting herself.

"Almost like it was me," she said. "I feel for her, all right."

The cow immediately twisted about and began licking at the membrane around her calf, pulling it off with her teeth, then licking the wet head and body, lowing to her baby, the calf bawling back in turn.

"They'll recognize each other now," Ryan explained to Barry. "You put 'em out in the herd together, the mother will recognize her calf and the calf can find its mother."

Lon Walker leaned down to unfasten the chains.

"Pretty miraculous," he said. "Feel it every time. Nothin' beats life, that's for sure."

"The animals know where they belong," Mother added. "They know their place, and life goes along peaceful, one day to the next. They live the way God intended."

And end up steak on somebody's table, Ryan was thinking, half smiling. He decided not to tell them that Barry was Polish.

He didn't have to. It was much later, when the boys were finishing up their report, the dogs at their feet, that Gil came in at last to have his dinner. He stopped in the doorway and stared at Barry. Then wordlessly he began dishing up a bowl of stew.

"Gil, this is Barry from school," Ryan said. "We're finishing up our report."

"Dubinsky?" asked Gil.

"That's right," said Barry.

Gil reached for a spoon in the drawer and took his dinner into the other room.

Ten

The first big storm of the season was a blinding, swirling, writhing snow, inhaled with every breath. In fields, bands of hay had been left unmowed to serve as snow fences, yet drifts five and six feet high piled up against barns and sheds—closed the schools till the roads were cleared, then formed jagged walls of grungy white along the highway.

Lon Walker and Gil and Ryan went out early each morning to break up the ice in the water troughs so the cattle could drink. They tackled their own trough first, then went over to Hank's and shoveled the ice off the troughs in the holding lots.

"I would sure like to be out of here and gone," Gil said once as the three hacked away at the ice, using whatever tools were handy. The wind was so strong, they had to lean against it.

Lon Walker glanced over at him. "'Spect every cowhand who ever lived felt the same sometime in winter. Spring comes, it's a different story."

"Not for me," said Gil. "I think what I'd like to do is be a trucker, own my own rig."

"You know what it costs to buy one of those big trucks?" his father asked. "You could buy some kind of palace out here for what one of those rigs would cost you! You gotta start small, Gil! How many times I got to tell you that? You'd have to rent a truck to start."

"And be under someone else's thumb? No, thanks," Gil told him. He was jabbing at the ice so hard with the shovel that Ryan had to move over to make room.

Lon stopped hacking for a moment and studied Gil's face. "Then you'd have to work somewhere else so you could make enough money to buy one. Trouble with you, Gil, you can't ever see anything through. Nothin' seems to stick. Remember couple summers ago you and Sid and another guy bought that gold detector and headed for California? Got as far as Nevada and your money ran out."

Now Gil was getting hot under the collar. "I told you Sid's car broke down—would have cost all we had and more to fix it. Nothing to do *but* hitchhike back. That greaseball mechanic—him and the guy who ran the station—they had that place sewed up. You look around and half the town was greaseballs and the rest were Indian."

Lon shook his head and rested a moment, leaning on the handle of his spade. "It's always somebody else holding you back, isn't it? Always somebody else to blame. . . ."

Gil simply plunged his shovel into the ice as hard as it would go and stalked off, his boots crunching on the frozen snow.

On school days when it snowed, only Gil ventured out in the four-by-four to drive Ryan and Charlene to their bus stops, and picked them up in the afternoons. Weekends, the TV came on in the mornings and stayed on all day.

One afternoon Ryan was helping Freddy put together his latest rocket warrior when the phone rang, Charlene answered, and five seconds later, the house was filled with a piercing scream. Ryan whirled around to see her standing with the telephone still dangling in her hand. Mother, making sauce out of the last of autumn's apples, turned from the sink. Midnight and Sergeant, who had been sleeping in one corner of the kitchen, raised their heads.

"Charlene?" Mother said.

But it took the family only a moment to discover that it had been a scream of pure joy.

"I'm one of the nominees for Junior Rodeo Queen!" Charlene cried, putting both hands on her cheeks. "They just posted the list in the feed store, Eleanor said. There's eight of us, and they're going to announce the winner next March."

"Now isn't that something!" said Doris Walker, pleased.

"Sound like a stuck pig! Thought you'd had your throat slit or something!" Gil told her, coming up from the basement.

Ryan, who liked most to hang around the chute boss at rodeos, trying to predict how each animal would react when the chute gate opened, now tried to imagine what it would be like to see his sister crowned queen of the community rodeo. Every year people dropped their suggestions for Junior Rodeo Queen in a box at the feed store, and the eight high school girls who got the most votes were the nominees. The winner often went on to become rodeo queen at the state fair, which meant she was in the running for Miss Rodeo America.

The eight girls would be watched carefully for four months by three local judges, but the girls wouldn't know who the judges were. At the rodeo in May, the lucky girl would gallop around the ring in a sparkly top and jeans, holding the American flag. It might be sort of nice to go to school and say it was his sister, Ryan thought. Something to talk about, anyway. On the other hand, if she didn't make it . . . Ryan hated to think what life would be like around Walker's Crossing if Charlene didn't make queen. For the next four months, though, she would have to be on her best behavior, and he sure had no quarrel with that.

For the next hour Charlene was on the phone, copying down the list of nominees, calling her friends and squealing, it seemed, on every other word. When she finally hung up, she pranced around the room, waving the list, and Gil managed to get it away from her to see who else had been nominated.

"Hey! Dee Gibbons! I know her. Cute little blonde, right? Jamie Young, Sid's sister. You got some stiff competition, Char. You better brush up on your riding, practice your barrel racing." He ran his finger on down the list, then paused. "You see this one? Maria Palacios? How'd she get on there?"

"She's a junior. Why shouldn't she?" said Charlene.

"Don't tell me you didn't notice, Char. She's a taco."

"So? I didn't make the rules."

"So how you going to feel if she turns out to be rodeo queen? It wasn't Mexicans who built the West, it was us."

"What does that have to do with anything?" Charlene asked.

Ryan gave a little laugh. "'Course, it wasn't exactly ours to begin with."

"Well, it sure as heck wasn't Mexico's!" said Gil. "Wasn't Mexicans who wrote the Constitution. So why should there be a taco rodeo queen, I ask you, riding around the ring holding the American flag?"

Ryan didn't know the answer to that one, and neither did Charlene. Gil asked a lot of questions lately about things Ryan hadn't thought of before, and half the time, anyway, they made sense. The rest, Ryan wasn't sure.

The third calf was born without complications, and there was only one more to go. But now something had been hanging around the pasture and barn. Lon Walker saw tracks in the snow.

"Think we got a cougar looking for calf meat," he said that weekend. "Heard the horses carrying on last night—they must have caught wind of something."

"Why don't we lock the calves in the barn?" Ryan suggested.

"Can do it for now, but if the cougar gets hungry enough, he'll take one of the cows," his father told him. "Can't keep 'em in there forever. Hank's going to put two of his men on night patrol for a while for the herds, but just my luck, the cougar'll come here."

"Now that's a job for the Mountain Patriots," said Gil. "We'll sit up all night and take care of that cougar, it decides to come around."

"I'd appreciate that," said Dad, sounding pleased.

"Let me sit, too," said Ryan excitedly. "It's Friday. I don't have to go to school tomorrow."

Gil started to say no, then reconsidered. "You think you could shoot straight? Don't want you shootin' the wrong thing."

"You put a can out there on a fence post, I can blow it away in one shot," Ryan bragged.

"Okay, then. Maybe you'll learn a little somethin' in the bargain."

Ryan was glad to be included. He liked the thought of taking his .22 out after dark and sitting around waiting for the big cat to show.

As it turned out, three of the men in Sheldon's outfit came over. They figured that three plus Gil and

Ryan ought to be enough to kill a cougar. The five of them sat behind the barn with a freshly killed chicken some fifty feet off.

"It'll smell that, all right," Big Ed said. He was the largest and heaviest of the men. Sid was the one who shaved his head, Ryan remembered, and Sonny the friend with the curly hair.

The moon was bright, and the chicken was out in the open where anything moving would be detected. The calves were in the barn tonight, though the fourth cow in the west pasture was close to delivery, and Dad was keeping an eye on her. Get a cow in the act of birthing—that would be an easy banquet for a cougar.

The men were seated with their backs to a stone wall, downwind of the dead chicken, rifles cocked and resting on their knees.

"Any one of us sees him, we give Ryan the signal and he turns on the spotlight. It's all set and ready," said Sid.

They waited, all but Ryan with a pinch of Copenhagen between lip and gum.

"What we need is some of them headlamps that let you see in the dark," said Big Ed. "I hear some of the militia boys got those."

"What we really need," said Sid, "is that AR-15 assault rifle, Gil. Where you got it?"

"Over at Sheldon's. He's keeping the guns."

"Heck, I could turn it into a fully automatic, I had the time. Cougar wouldn't have a chance."

"And the ATF would be on your tail quicker'n you

could say ZOG," said Big Ed, shooting a stream of tobacco two yards away.

"What's ATF?" asked Ryan. "What's ZOG?"

"Hey, maybe we got a young recruit here," said Sid. "I'll tell you: ATF stands for the Alcohol, Tobacco, and Firearms Agency that wants to control your life, your mind. Tell you what you can drink, what you can chew, and what you can shoot."

"Mom," said Ryan, and the men chuckled. Ryan liked being able to make them laugh.

Sid went on: "What they'd really like to do is take away your beer, your tobacco, and your guns, and ZOG is behind it."

"Zionist Occupation Government," explained Gil, "because that's who's running Congress now, only ninety-nine percent of Americans don't know it."

"Babylon. That's what *I* call the government," said Sid.

Ryan didn't know what to think, and when he made no comment, Sonny got into the act: "The Jews have taken over the banks, Ryan, the courts, every branch of government, and that's what groups like ours are all about. We all got the same purpose—to rescue the U.S. Constitution from the Jews and give the land back to the people who wrote the Bill of Rights." His voice rose as he warmed to the topic. "We don't want to overthrow the government, but we sure as heck would like to restore it."

Gil poked him: "Keep your voice down; you'll scare off the cat."

"We're like the minutemen back when our country was new," said Big Ed. "It's like my old lady says: Everybody is a potential FBI person. My chamber's always loaded, the hammer's back."

It wasn't a joke anymore.

Sid said, "It all comes down to what kind of a man you aim to be, Ryan. You gonna be the kind that if a foreigner takes a good, admiring look at your sister or your girlfriend, you're gonna smile and say, 'Sure. Go ahead, have a taste while you're at it'? Or you the kind that'll show you have some guts, that'll say, 'You son-of-a-bee, that was one look too many,' and calmly put a gun to his eyeball and shoot."

"Ah, c'mon, Sid, we're not in the assassination business," said Gil. "All we're doing, Ryan, is putting people on notice that here in this little piece of the West, the White Race is in charge. Up here we've still got a chance."

"You ought to join," urged Sonny.

Ryan sat feeling the cold metal of the spotlight against his knees. He liked the idea of protecting Sheila, Freddy . . . He felt sure that he was sitting with at least four of the men who had ridden to Teepee's on Halloween night in sheets and hoods. But, as someone said, they'd just been making a point. When Thomas Jefferson and Benjamin Franklin signed the Declaration of Independence, they must have been looked on at the time as rebels, too. Sid and Big Ed talked tough, maybe, but what if they were right? Maybe the Jews *were* taking over.

116

"What . . . what would I have to do to join?" Ryan asked, his mouth dry.

"Be a little older than you are, for one thing." Gil smiled.

"It's a secret ceremony out in a field," said Sonny. "But there isn't any reason you can't be a junior cadet. Take an oath right now, if you want, with us as your witnesses."

"What kind of an oath?" asked Ryan.

"An oath any red-blooded American man would be proud to take: that you'll defend your home with your life; your woman—when you get one—with your life; that you'll never betray one of your patriot brothers, even under torture," Big Ed told him.

What could be wrong with that? What could be wrong with vowing to protect Sheila, for example? Charlene, even? And he wouldn't ever betray his friends, so why not?

The men waited. Ryan could hear Sonny's breathing beside him. Up above, a million stars looked down on him, all witness to this night. His heart pounded.

"All right," he said.

Big Ed recited the oath, line by line, and Ryan repeated it after him: ". . . that I will never betray one of my brothers, even under torture or threat of death," he said.

Eleven

They did not kill the cougar.

"Must have got wind of us, or heard us talkin'," Gil said.

But at Hank's the next day, Ryan found out that Moe had killed it. The cougar had attacked a calf, and Moe put a bullet through its neck.

"I didn't like to do it," he said. "Those big cats, they usually don't get so close. Food must be scarce for the wild ones."

"Ryan, your family having a big Thanksgiving this year?" Debbie asked as she prepared to go with the men and distribute hay by sled to the far corners of the holding lots.

"Nothing special, I guess," he told her.

"Well, after you get through eating at home, you're still hungry, stop in over here. Making a pecan pie just for you," she said.

He grinned.

On Sunday, when Ryan met Matt at Teepee's, Matt grabbed his arm and whispered, "Sheila's in a booth. Come over with me and talk to her."

"What? How do you know she's not waiting for someone?" Ryan said.

"I don't. How do you know she's not waiting for *us*?"

"*Us? You*, you mean. *You* go sit with her. I wouldn't know what to say."

"Come on, Ryan. It's easier with two."

Ryan felt dizzy. Sitting in the school cafeteria with a girl was one thing. Sitting in a booth was another. Aunt Peg was smiling at them over by the counter, though, so Ryan took a deep breath and followed Matt to the booth, sliding in beside him across from Sheila. She had the shiniest dark hair Ryan had ever seen. Her black sweater was patterned with little white sheep, and she wore a red shirt underneath.

"Well, look what the wind blew in," said Sheila. "I just ordered myself a malted."

"Aunt Peg makes the best," Ryan told her, then realized his feet were all the way under her seat and bumping into hers. He withdrew them at once, and his knee jogged the table.

"That's your aunt?" Sheila asked.

"Yeah." Ryan found his face reddening; he didn't know why.

"So . . . what did you order for me?" asked Matt.

Sheila laughed. "For *you?* How did I know you were coming?"

"Who else would you be waiting for?" asked Matt.

Sheila rolled her eyes.

Aunt Peg came over. "I've got one chocolate malt coming up; what'll you guys have?" she asked.

"A malt for me," Ryan told her.

"Coffee," said Matt. "I'll take it black."

Ryan smirked. He'd never known Matt to like coffee.

But Aunt Peg didn't even blink. "You got it," she said, and left.

Ryan could not believe it when he saw Matt, grinning, reach across the table and put his hand over Sheila's. She gave him a quizzical frown and pulled away.

"What's wrong?" Matt asked.

She laughed. "Nothing! Just don't go so fast."

Matt appeared to be studying her for a minute, and then, resting his chin on one hand, he began inching his other hand across the tabletop in slow motion, like letting his fingers walk the yellow pages.

Sheila giggled. "What are you *doing?*"

"Going slower," he said, and this time, when his fingers reached her hand, she kept it there, and his hand closed over hers, but they were still laughing.

Ryan was beside himself with envy. How did the guy *do* it? But Sheila withdrew her hand when Aunt Peg came back with the coffee and malteds.

"Enjoy!" she said, and left them alone.

"You here with your folks?" Ryan asked Sheila.

"Only Dad. He's having his clutch adjusted. Said he'd be here for a while, so I decided to ride along."

Afterward, Ryan couldn't remember much of anything they'd said at the booth. They'd fooled around with the plastic straws, and finally got up to wander around the general store. Ryan looked at leather jackets, and Sheila tried on Western hats from the men's rack. They came down over her eyes, but she wore them at a tipsy angle that made her even more attractive, Ryan thought. He and Matt put another hat on top of the one she was wearing, then another, laughing, until seven hats were balanced tipsily on her head.

At last they saw a man signaling over by the door, and Sheila introduced her father.

"Well, *you're* the tall one, aren't you?" Mr. Harrison said, shaking hands with Ryan and Matt. Ryan couldn't think of a single reply. It was such a stupid remark, really, as though Ryan had chosen his own height.

Mr. Harrison turned to Sheila. "Anything else you need to do here? Shall we hit the road?"

"I'm done," she said.

"Nice to meet you, Ryan . . . Matt," the man said, and started across the lot toward his car.

"See you in school," Sheila said, and left.

Ryan felt like he'd been a jerk with her father, but Matt was still beaming with the success of his encounter.

"I don't know what you need me for," said Ryan.

"Well, maybe next time I won't," Matt told him.

Ryan had promised he'd go to a Patriots meeting, so he set out one Sunday evening, just before dusk. Gil said he'd meet him there at the Sheldons' after he finished at Teepee's.

It was blowing snow. The wind was so strong that the dry, white stuff seemed to slide along over bare ground, caught at last by fences, the sides of barns, piling up against tree trunks, and creeping its way up the silos.

Ryan walked across the barren fields with his head down so as not to lose his hat. The wind was in his face until he rounded a bluff, and then it hit him sideways. He grabbed his Stetson to keep it on.

Ray Sheldon was out by the old frame barn when Ryan got there—one of the few wooden barns left, most were metal—doing repairs to his backhoe under a light he'd rigged up. Ryan waved as he walked up on their porch, stomping the snow off his feet. It was an old house, in keeping with the barn, with four rooms and a loft.

The two-year-old twins, David and John, were squabbling loudly over a toy when Ryan went inside, but stopped as soon as they saw him, ambling over to grin and try to get his attention.

"Hello, Ryan. You're the first one here," Mrs. Sheldon called from the far end of the room where she was stuffing wood in the potbellied stove. "Matt'll be in in a minute. He's on the other side of the house filling the wood bin. Been busy over at your place, I hear."

"Yeah, we've been calving," Ryan said. He sat down on the edge of a chair and amused the twins by picking up small toys from the floor and dropping them, one at a time, down the fronts of their overalls. The boys shrieked delightedly as the toys fell out the bottoms of their pant legs.

"Sure am glad to have you here at the meeting," Mrs. Sheldon went on. "It's not just the men who are going to look out for us, it's the job of you boys, too. You see things around here—at school and at Teepee's—that we don't, and it'll take the strength of every man, woman, and child when the Apocalypse comes."

Ryan wasn't sure what she was talking about. He remembered an old movie called *Apocalypse Now* but couldn't quite remember what it was about. War, maybe.

"War?" he asked.

"Armageddon—that's another name for it. When it gets here, you'll know it." She came over and sat across from him, leaning forward, elbows resting on her knees. "As sure as anything, Ryan, there's an Antichrist, and he could take any form at all—a man, a boy, a woman, even—ready to strike, to start the conflagration just when we're most vulnerable. We're just trying to live like the Bible says, and keep ourselves separate from them that would destroy us."

Ryan had never felt comfortable with Matt's

mother, the way she was always preaching at him. He tried to appear pleasant, and went on playing with the twins, who were intent now on stuffing little trucks and cars down the inside of Ryan's jacket. He playfully fended them off. But Mrs. Sheldon went on:

"I got my own pledge to keep, and that's to see that my three boys marry into good white stock and keep our race pure, like God intended."

Matt came in just then with an armload of wood and dropped it in the wood box by the stove. Ryan quickly stood up, glad for the interruption. He didn't know his Bible well enough to understand Armageddon, but it was hard to imagine any kind of war here in Wyoming. If there was an invasion, though, they could count on him. All he could imagine were cattle rustlers, big time. City folk needing the beef for food. Something like that ever came about, he'd be out there on the Saddlebow, his rifle ready, along with Hank and Dennis.

"Want to go out back now?" Matt said. "Big Ed just got here."

"Sure," said Ryan.

"The newsletter came," Mrs. Sheldon called after them. "Take some copies with you."

Ryan picked one up from the pile near the door and followed Matt to the barn.

Kevin hadn't come this time, but Gil walked in wearing his flak jacket, and after Richard Sheldon turned on the kerosene heater, the men recited a pledge of allegiance, first to the United States, and then to each other. Matt stood with his hand over his heart, eyes on his dad, who was wearing army fatigues. When they sat down, he and Ryan took two barrels shoved up against one wall. The men had their choice of seats from a motley bunch of folding chairs, a wooden bench, and an old rusty glider.

For the first few minutes the talk was of the van Sonny had purchased the week before, and then Matt's father said, "Okay, let's get down to business. What we're concentrating on tonight is how not to be a sitting duck. We're not going to be holed up in some cabin waiting for government thugs to come and take our guns. We're not going to be locked in some compound waiting for government tanks to tear down the walls. If there's going to be another Waco, another Ruby Ridge, it'll be us that fires the first shot. They come after us, we'll be ready."

"You got that right," said Sonny.

"This doesn't mean we're looking for a fight; we're not going off half cocked. But when you're on the government's hit list, they're not fooling."

"Why are we on their hit list?" Ryan whispered to Matt. "What have we done?"

"Nothing. We've just got guns to protect ourselves, that's all, and that's what drives 'em nuts," Matt whispered back.

"So what are we going to do?" asked Sid.

"That's something we've got to decide," said Sheldon. "I'll tell you what the fellas down in Georgia did, before they got careless and got themselves arrested.

125

They were filling bomb casings with explosives. ATF's coming down the road out there, you could pull one out, hit it, and throw it."

"I figure April's when the feathers'll hit the fan," said Gil. "They're not going to let us forget the Oklahoma City bombing. They'll be after every gun in the country, make an example of us."

Big Ed disagreed. "That's what they want you to think. Get everybody thinking April, and they'll surprise you. My guess is it'll be March. Try to catch us off guard."

Sonny propped his feet on an old radiator. "I say stick to high ground. It's the only way to get the drop on the ATF or the hordes that'll be coming this way when the riots begin. I think we should be pooling our money and build us a compound up on a hill somewhere."

"Yeah, and who's got that kind of money? You?" asked Sid.

Richard Sheldon shook his head. "That's somewhere down the road," he said impatiently. "What we need are topographical maps, shortwave radios, police scanners—stuff like that. What we've got to be concentrating on now is preparedness in the home, in your truck—wherever you happen to be. Make sure your weapons are chambered. The government's getting ready for something. I don't know what it is, but we're reaching the boiling point, that's a fact. Just remember that we're in the right; it's the government that's immoral."

Several men began talking at once about self-defense, but Sheldon took over again:

". . . there's even a right way to go to the bathroom," he said, and—just as Ryan, grinning, was about to nudge Matt—he added, "Don't laugh. You turn your back at a urinal, you're a target. Ever think of that? The proper technique is to go in a stall and sit on the toilet with the pistol between your legs, ready to fire on anyone who invades your space."

The men laughed a little awkwardly. Ryan wished that Matt didn't take it so seriously. He sat there like a soldier at attention, as if to tell Ryan that if he was too young for this kind of thing, he could leave.

There was a weapons demonstration next. Big Ed showed the men how they could use a handkerchief to improve their accuracy with a revolver. "You wrap one corner of the handkerchief around the revolver grip, see, then you grip it with your hand and take the opposite corner of the handkerchief and clasp it in your teeth. Now . . . aim the gun out from your body, strain with your mouth and your arm so you have two points of support. Like so . . ."

Everyone had a technique that he wanted to show, and Ryan's mind began to wander. Actually, he felt a little sleepy, and was embarrassed when Matt saw him yawn. For all the kidding around that Matt did with Sheila at school, he didn't find anything funny about this. He seemed to be growing more like his father every day. Dead set. Dead serious.

Matt's dad was talking again: "What you've got to

remember is never to be anywhere without a backup weapon, and if it's a choice between a rifle and a scattergun, I say choose the rifle. It doesn't have to be a bull gun with a ten-power scope—an ordinary deer rifle will do the job. . . ."

Ryan felt another yawn tugging at his chin, and he pulled the newsletter out of his pocket to focus on that. This time in the box at the bottom it read: *Food for Thought: God has a plan for homosexuals. AIDS is the beginning.*

The first column began with *a mighty warm welcome to the Mountain Patriots' Association over there in the Bighorn Basin, who agree with our philosophy right down the line. You can count on us, boys, if the going gets tough, because when the going gets tough, the tough get going! We'll be there!"*

The first article began with Bible verses from Matthew 24: *When ye therefore shall see the abomination of desolation, spoken of by Daniel the prophet, stand in the holy place: Then let them which be in Judaea flee into the mountains.*

What did it mean? Ryan wondered.

Myles A. Reddick, Editor, had the answer: *When it's time to divide the sheep from the goats, your heart has to be 100 percent in the right place. Not 98 percent. Not 99 percent, because that last 1 percent is going to be the crack that lets the mud people through.*

So who are the mud people? Ryan wondered, and once again, the newsletter had the answer: *White people are the true descendants of the ancient Israelites, in direct line from Adam and Eve. The Jews, on the other hand, descended from Cain, who was not born of Adam and Eve, but of Eve and the serpent. Cain's children fled into the woods, mated with the beasts, and produced the nonwhites. The mud races.*

So what are we required to do? the newsletter went on. *If you read the fine print, if you read between the lines, it's as plain as the nose on your face:*

1. *Post soldiers all along the Mexican border to stop the immigrants.*
2. *Quarantine all AIDS patients, let them die off naturally.*
3. *Kill the scum drug dealers.*
4. *No special privileges to Indians or blacks just because they think they were mistreated once. We were all mistreated somewhere down the line.*
5. *Turn over the whole continent of Africa to the blacks and ship them back, at our expense. Better to pay their steerage than welfare the rest of their lives.*

Man, Ryan thought, folding the paper and sticking it back in his pocket. *This is really getting heavy!* He didn't even *know* any blacks or Jews. The only Mexican he knew was Moe Morales. He didn't know anyone with AIDS, either, or any drug dealers. Maybe if he ever met some of the mud people and had a fight with them or something, he'd understand what folks were fired up about, but right now it seemed like a lot of energy wasted over nothing. Still, Richard Sheldon must know something. You didn't move your family all the way up from California and buy guns and stuff unless you had a reason. He stole another look at Matt, straightened his shoulders, and tried to pay attention.

Charlene went to a basketball game after school on Thursday, and when she came home, she threw her jacket down on a chair in disgust.

"It sure is hard to be nice to everybody when people act like they did at the game," she complained. "There's this new player—Ben Schwartz—and every time he made a basket, some of the kids booed. Our own team! Somebody said he was Jewish."

"It's a Jew name," said Gil.

"Well, I just pretended like I didn't hear them. Other kids turned and glared at them, but I just went on cheering and clapping no matter who on our team scored, and then I wondered if I should have done that—if one of the judges was watching. It's really hard to play Miss Rodeo when I don't know exactly what I'm supposed to do, and especially when I don't even know if I'll win."

"Well, I wouldn't boo anybody, not even a Jew, but I sure wouldn't clap or cheer one, either," said her mother. "There's a difference between being downright mean to somebody and not giving him any encouragement. Let's say I was a clerk in a store and a black woman comes in to buy herself some shoes. I wouldn't refuse to sell 'em to her, but I sure wouldn't put 'em on her feet. You wouldn't find me being chummy with them. Wouldn't bring 'em home to eat at our table or anything."

"The important thing is they get the message that we're in charge," said Gil. "Let's say the Schwartz guy turns out to be a star—makes all the points, that kind of thing. Everybody's friend. He'll be on the telephone to his friends in New York City, saying, 'Come out West. Great place to live,' and first thing you know, we'll have a phone directory full of Weinsteins and Goldbergs and a lot of little Jews running around on Saturdays with beanies on their heads."

Freddy laughed. *"Beanies!"* he said, and laughed again.

Just so they don't come hanging around the Saddle-bow, Ryan thought. He did his homework after dinner, then settled down in front of the TV, the largest of the gray tabbies in his lap. At seven-thirty, Mother put Freddy to bed, then took out the little patchwork quilt she was stitching for Martha Sheldon, who was expecting another child. Gil had gone out, but around nine he returned, kicked off his boots, and plunked quickly down on the sofa beside Ryan, feet on the coffee table.

"Anybody come to the door, I was here all evening," he said, half smiling.

"Gil, what did you do?" asked Dad, looking up from his seed catalog.

"Relax. We didn't hurt anyone."

"Then what are you going on about?" Mother wanted to know.

"Nothing. Forget it. Just making a statement, that's all," Gil said.

When Ryan went to bed, Gil still hadn't told them, and all Dad said was, "Some kind of foolishness, you can bet."

Ryan learned about it at school the next day. Spray-painted on one wall of the high school, he heard, next to the gym, was a huge Nazi swastika and the words NO ROOM FOR JEWS.

Twelve

"I can't believe that happened here," said Sheila.

She was still talking about it at lunchtime. Everyone was. It was the talk of the middle school all morning. Sheila and her friend Amy had joined the boys at their table in the cafeteria, and she angrily bit into her sandwich.

"Oh, it didn't hurt anybody," Matt said. "Just somebody saying how he feels, that's all."

"That's *all?*" said Amy.

"It's still a free country last time I checked," said Kevin. "People still have a right to like who they want—*dis*like somebody if they want."

"I'll bet whoever wrote that doesn't even know that basketball player," said Sheila.

"You don't have to know him to know about him. For one thing, white people give off positive electrons. Jews and other races give off negative," Kevin told her.

"What?" said Sheila.

"Jews are white," said Amy.

"Not really. You know the test for racial purity?" Kevin went on. "If you can blush—show blood in the face."

"You guys are full of it," Sheila declared. "It won't be long before we all have check marks by our names. They'll find something wrong with *all* of us."

"You're pretty, you can stay," Matt joked.

"Thank you very much!" she replied, but she wasn't pleased.

And Kevin said, "You don't have to worry about *your* ancestors."

"What's the big deal about ancestors?" she shot back.

"Harrison—that's English, right?"

"For your information," Sheila told him, "my father's ancestors are from England, and my mom's Greek. Helen Palamas. Is that good enough for you?"

Ryan went on eating until he was conscious, suddenly, of the silence around the table. Matt, who was sitting beside Sheila, turned and stared at her. "You're Greek?"

"Fifty percent." She studied him, her eyes laughing. "You have a problem with that?"

Ryan was surprised to see the blood rising to Matt's face. *The sign of racial purity,* he thought jokingly. But

Matt wasn't looking at Sheila any longer; he was staring down at his tray.

She nudged him playfully. "You have a problem with that?" she asked again, bending her head to look up into his face.

And finally, still without looking at her, Matt put his sandwich back on his tray and stood up. "I guess I do," he said and, to Ryan's astonishment, carried his tray over to the tray table, then left the cafeteria. The group stared after him.

"What's the matter with *him?*" Amy said.

Ryan tried to remember the names of the twelve Aryan nations that Gil had told him about—the "acceptable" countries, the "right" countries: the U.S., Great Britain, then DIG and SNIFF with an H and an S left over: Denmark, Iceland, Germany, Sweden, Norway, Italy, France, Finland . . . Holland and Spain. No Greece.

He kept staring at Sheila, wondering if she was changing before his eyes—if she looked more foreign than he imagined.

"So what's wrong with Greece? It's right next to Italy, isn't it?" he asked Kevin, laughing a little and trying to turn the whole thing into a joke. Still, his eyes were fixed on Sheila's dark eyes, her hair, the faint, soft fuzz above her lip.

Kevin, however, didn't answer. He picked up his milk carton, drained it, then stood and picked up his own tray. "You coming, Ryan?" he asked.

Ryan couldn't believe what was happening. He

looked at Sheila and saw the shock in her eyes that he had even hesitated. "No," he said. "I'm not coming."

Kevin walked away.

"Can you *believe* that?" said Amy. "Can you *believe* that? All because her mother's Greek. Has everyone gone nuts?"

But Ryan was conscious of Sheila's eyes on him, her questioning look.

"A bunch of us are going to the high school tomorrow to help paint over the graffiti," she said at last, trying to overcome her own humiliation. Ryan knew it was his trial by fire. "Will you go with us?"

He had to say something. "Yes," he told her.

He was as tense as a mustang all day. *To go or not to go.* Math he failed big time; couldn't concentrate. In history, Mr. Phillips had the Western states listed on the blackboard, and was going over the dates that each had become part of the Union. And even though this was Ryan's favorite class, his favorite teacher, he scarcely heard.

"You going to the high school tomorrow?" Barry asked him later.

"Yeah. I'm not sure how I'll get there, though."

"Want us to pick you up? I'm pretty sure Dad could drive."

"That'd be great," Ryan told him, and was surprised that his voice came out shaky.

Matt stared at him coldly. "You're making a mistake, Walker," he said. "A big, big mistake."

"Maybe," Ryan replied. "Maybe not."

Ryan wished he'd sounded more forceful, but his head was about to burst. Sheila was half Greek, she said, and this information, which seemed so monstrous to Matt, only left him confused. He'd tried to study her unobtrusively that afternoon as she sat across from him in English—her thick, dark hair, the heavy brows above her eyes, the way she smiled, moved her hands . . . She was the same Sheila. He'd come to know her too well to think of her in any other way. But he didn't have to marry her or anything. Didn't even have to think about stuff like that. So he'd marry someone from one of the twelve Aryan nations when it came time. No big deal. He wasn't muddying the gene pool, betraying his race.

He called Hank that evening and told him he couldn't come over on Saturday.

"Hey, no problem!" Hank said. "It's quiet here now. You just wait till calving time."

"I know," said Ryan. "We've been through that over here."

Barry and his father picked him up the next morning. Ryan went outside when the car pulled up, and slid into the backseat.

Mr. Dubinsky was a tall, large-boned man with a boyish smile, showing lots of teeth. He reached around and shook Ryan's hand. "How ya' doing?" he said. "Nice of you guys to help out. I know the folks over at the high school appreciate it. Best to stop things like this before they get out of hand. Show your support." The car started forward.

"I brought some sandpaper," said Barry. "I don't know if it's going to help, though."

Mr. Dubinsky shook his head. "Strange, isn't it? With all the problems there are in the world, some folks put their energies into taking out after a high school kid because of his name."

Ryan didn't answer. He felt as though his head—his brain, anyway—was slowly turning a hundred and eighty degrees, and it almost made him dizzy.

There was a small crowd at the high school. The wind was sharp, and the sky had a layered look of white and gray. Already someone was on a ladder, sanding away at the hateful words on the wooden planks. In fact, there were too many willing workers, and not quite enough graffiti to go around, but everyone seemed to want to take part.

Ryan took a sheet of sandpaper and attacked the swastika. Each push of the paper seemed to increase his resolve. It was as though he were scraping away something in himself that he didn't like—didn't even understand, really.

More people arrived, among them a cluster of young men who stood off to one side, watching but not participating. They weren't exactly heckling. Chuckling from time to time, perhaps. Ryan didn't recognize any of them, but he was glad Gil wasn't there.

An arm reached for a spot just above him, attacking

the top of the swastika, and Ryan looked over to see Mr. Phillips beside him. And then he paused and stared, because Mr. Phillips was wearing a yarmulke.

"Hello, Ryan," the teacher said, and his face was grave as he put muscle into attacking the paint on the building.

Ryan's hand, however, had almost stopped moving. Facts were coming at him too fast, almost, to decipher. Phillips was Jewish. This was Saturday, his Sabbath. He, Ryan, was standing here beside a Jew, attacking a swastika.

The sight of Mr. Phillips in his yarmulke seemed to agitate the young men on the sidelines.

"Hey!" one of them called. "What you doing all that work for? Somebody could put it right back on again." The other men ducked their heads and smiled.

The high school principal, up on a ladder, turned to face them. "Well, don't let that somebody be you," he said.

"As many times as they put it on, we'll take it off," Mr. Phillips said quietly to Ryan. "Thanks for helping. My grandfather is smiling at us now, I'm sure."

"Your grandfather?" Ryan looked over at the crowd on the sidelines.

"Not here. He died in forty-three. In Auschwitz."

Ryan continued to sand away at the paint. "I guess we don't have too many Jews out here," he said finally.

Phillips smiled. "I guess not. But this is still America. We're supposed to be able to go anywhere we want

139

in this land. *Everyone.* No guarantee what kind of welcome we'll get, of course."

Ryan thought of what Gil had said about New York Jews coming out here buying up land, raising property values, driving the ranchers out.

"Did you come out here from New York City?" he asked, wondering. *Jew York,* Gil often called it.

"Connecticut."

Close enough. "Are you going to buy a house?" Ryan asked.

"I already have. I love Wyoming."

Another car pulled up, and a photographer from the county weekly got out, camera bag slung over one shoulder. He crouched down on the sidewalk facing the gym wall and adjusted his lens. Ryan's first thought was to turn his back. Then he caught Sheila's smile and, after that, he didn't care.

It was in social studies, not history, that the incident was brought up again on Monday. For several weeks they had been studying the criminal justice system, learning the difference between capital crimes, felonies, and misdemeanors, and reading about how various cities and states were reducing crime and rehabilitating prisoners.

Matt raised his hand, and Miss Wells, a small young woman with large round glasses, nodded in his direction as she leaned against her desk, feet crossed at the ankles.

"I've got a really simple solution," Matt offered. His voice sounded unnatural to Ryan. Too loud. Too cold.

"It's a well-known fact that blacks are mentally re-tarded"—There were loud objections from the class, but Matt barreled on—"and commit most of the crimes. If we would just expel them from this coun-try—even if we only stopped any more from coming in—we'd see crime go down in a big way."

Astonished exclamations peppered the air, but Miss Wells remained unflustered. "What's your source? Where do you get your information?" she asked.

"Everybody knows it," Kevin called out. "People just don't talk about it, that's all."

"You'll never see the truth in any of the big newspa-pers because the Jews control the media, and they don't want you to know," Matt continued. "All the . . ."

Jeers drowned him out.

"I don't get it," said Ryan, looking right at Matt. "Why should Jews be sticking up for blacks?"

"Because blacks are their henchmen—they'll do whatever Jews tell them to do."

Some of the students stared at Matt in disbelief; others guffawed.

"You must have been one of the night riders at Teepee's on Halloween," someone called out.

"He's definitely out of the Dark Ages," Sheila said in disgust.

Matt ignored her. He kept his eyes focused on Miss Wells at the front of the room, and he seemed to Ryan like a soldier going into battle: He didn't exactly want to, maybe, but it was something he had to do. Had been taught to do.

141

"Okay, let's assume for a minute that there are statistics to back him up, class. Let's say Matt comes up with figures showing that, percentage wise, more blacks than whites commit crimes. What does this prove?" the teacher asked.

"That they're morally inferior," Matt replied.

More jeers.

"Hey, Matt!" called Amy. "What if somebody came up with a statistic that fewer men in Wyoming go to college than in most of the other states. Does that mean you're stupid?"

"Of course not." Matt faced the others with no expression at all. "There aren't that many colleges, for one thing, because there aren't that many cities in Wyoming. It's not the same."

Laughter.

"So you admit that circumstances play a part in the statistics, right?" asked Miss Wells. "Just as there might be circumstances in the lives of blacks, assuming your statistics were correct, that account for crime. Don't be misled by a false correlation. That's something we're going to talk more about next week."

"Maybe we should talk about prejudice and bigotry," said Sheila, anger in her voice. "It would be more to the point."

"That, too," said Miss Wells. "But I applaud Matt for bringing his ideas out in an open forum where he claims ownership of his views, unlike whoever wrote on the high school wall and was too cowardly to claim his belief. In this class, however, I require that you be able to support your ideas with facts. 'Everybody knows' is not a fact: It's an opinion. If you asked a group of four-year-olds, for example, how they know there is a Santa, and they answered that 'everybody knows,' they would be basing their belief on the opinions of their peers, but that still doesn't make Santa Claus exist. So if you'd like to bring data to class on clinical trials that determine blacks to be mentally retarded, Matt, I'll be glad to consider this as a topic for our next discussion."

Matt merely smiled. "You'll never get it in writing because the government won't let it out."

"Fact or opinion?" asked Miss Wells.

He shrugged. "The truth is out there. All you have to do is look around."

"Fact or opinion?" someone called out. Matt only shrugged again and turned to stare out the window. And Ryan knew that in giving up some of the friends he'd made and the status he'd had with Sheila, Matt had had to work twice as hard to convince himself he was right.

Scott Mullins tried to show his support. "Well, it would make an interesting experiment if you could set aside a whole region for a White Nation," he said. "Just to see what would happen to crime and everything. See if you didn't get superior leaders by keeping it white."

Miss Wells slowly took off her glasses. "I think it's already been done, Scott, and the leader was Adolf Hitler."

When Ryan got home from school that day, he saw

his picture in the county paper. Charlene was furious.

"Ryan, how *could* you?" she asked. "It's not just *me* the judges are looking at, it's every single member of my family. They're not going to elect a girl Junior Rodeo Queen if her family's off doing wild and crazy things that get their pictures in the paper."

"Seems like the wild and crazy part was putting that stuff on the wall of the high school in the first place," Ryan said, without looking at Gil.

Charlene suddenly broke into tears. "Don't you understand? We're not supposed to be controversial! I'm supposed to get along with everyone. Can't you, for the next few months, not do anything to call attention to this family? Or are you even going to get your pictures in the *Casper Star-Tribune*?" She included Gil in her plea, looking from him to Ryan.

"You don't see my picture in the paper," said Gil. "You don't see me out sanding off some American's God-given right to free speech. Maybe you don't happen to agree with it, but people have a right to express themselves."

"If they really want to express themselves, why don't they stand up in Teepee's parking lot, then, and say their piece?" Ryan shot back. "Why do they have to go crawling around at night like rats?"

He hardly realized what hit him. The next thing he knew, Gil loomed up before him, grabbed at his shirt and, despite Ryan's height, threw him to the floor and fell on top of him, his face dark.

"Stop it!" Lon Walker hollered into the room and

banged his hand against the wall. "Lunatics!" he bellowed, coming over and working to separate them.

Gil slowly raised himself off Ryan with a look of contempt. "You are some sorry sight," he growled. "What you doing, Ryan? Crossing over? I heard all about it from Matt. You're falling for a Greek girl, that's what's the matter with you."

"Shut up!" their father bellowed. "I swear I'll take the strap to you, Gil, if you don't shut your mouth."

"What's this?" Mother asked from the kitchen doorway. "Who's falling for a Greek girl? *You*, Ryan?" She hooted. "*You've* got a girlfriend?"

Ryan was getting to his feet. He felt like a giraffe trying to unfold his legs and stand. "So Sheila's half Greek, what of it?" he said. "And she's not my girlfriend."

The phone jangled—cutting across the argument—and Ryan wished it hadn't. Wished they could all stand right there and yell at each other till something in his head made sense.

Without even looking at the phone, still glaring at his sons, Lon Walker reached around and picked it up. "Yeah?" he said gruffly. And suddenly the anger went out of his face. "I'll be a son of a gun," he said. "We'll go right over."

He went immediately to the coatrack in the corner and pulled on his sheepskin jacket, then his hat. "Get your coats, boys," he said. "That was the sheriff. The Sheldons' barn is up in flames."

145

Thirteen

Richard Sheldon's backhoe was out in the yard, and his pickup parked by the house. But their old Dodge was beside the barn, too close to move, and about the time Lon drove his sons up the winding lane to the small house far back from the road, the gas tank of the Dodge blew. It went up in a roar.

The twins, David and John, stood off in the yard wailing, their jackets unzipped, but Matt's father was climbing a ladder at the side of the house, dragging wet blankets behind him to spread on the roof. Mrs. Sheldon emerged from inside with another armload of blankets, and Matt worked furiously as he dumped pail after pail of water on them.

Gil and Lon Walker climbed up after him, helping

to stretch out the blankets so that flying embers couldn't ignite the roof. Down below, Matt and Ryan stomped on the sparks that landed at their feet. At one point, Matt grabbed a bucket of water and threw it at the barn itself, but the fire lapped it up as though it were thirsty, and then, after sending up a thin gray plume of smoke, seemed to grow even stronger than before. Burning embers shot high into the air, some showering down only a few feet from the back porch.

"Oh, dear Jesus!" Martha Sheldon kept saying.

Another car arrived; men piled out. Already another family was inside the house, trying to coax water faster from the kitchen spigot.

"It's a write-off," one man said.

"Time to get out the wieners and buns," another murmured.

"The Coopers saw the smoke and called the sheriff on their cell phone," a friend told the Walkers. "Fire department's on the way, it ever gets here."

At last a siren sounded in the distance, and Ryan and Matt stood panting in the clearing, staring at the glowing orange and red frame of the Dodge back by the barn.

Richard Sheldon faced the fire, his arms in his singed sleeves dangling helplessly. "Too late," he said, shaking his head after a single tanker truck roared up the long, winding lane, and three volunteers leaped off. "It went up like a cardboard box."

The firefighters uncoiled their hoses, and trained their tanked water on the remains of the barn, sending up black roiling smoke that shut out the winter sunset. In less than a minute, the fire was under control.

Lon Walker grasped Matt's father sympathetically by the shoulder. "Buck up," he said. "You didn't have no cattle in it, and you still got your house, your wife and boys."

"Dick, you get you a phone up here, maybe things could move a little faster," one of the firemen said.

"Yeah, we got to hear it from a neighbor!" said another. "What if he hadn't been driving by? How you going to reach us?"

"*I* had to hear it from the sheriff!" Lon Walker said. "He figured me and my boys could get here faster'n anybody, but even that didn't do much good."

But Richard Sheldon walked over to the barn, the acrid smell of charred timber in the air, and kicked at the blackened frame of the Dodge. "You see what they did to me?" he said, looking around.

"What are you talking about, Dick?" Lon asked.

"You know who I mean. You know what this is about."

The fire inspector, who had been sloshing about in the remains of the barn, came over to where Mr. Sheldon was standing. He pointed to the blackened form of a metal heater, the charred wood of a bench beside it. "It was that kerosene heater you had out here. Somebody went and pushed a wooden bench up next to it, and nobody thought to turn the blamed thing off."

The other volunteers were nodding.

"Can't walk off and leave a heater on like that—

snug up against that old dry wood. Sure as anything that did it."

But Richard Sheldon just shook his head, his mouth set.

"I'm sorry about your barn and the car," Ryan said to Matt. Matt only turned and walked away.

The next Saturday, when Ryan got up and went to the kitchen, Dad was already tending to the calves, but Mother was on the phone. He jiggled a chair to dislodge a cat, and quietly poured himself some cereal.

". . . Well, *Gil* don't think it was an accident," his mother said. "No, he don't! He says this is just the way the ATF works—starts hounding a man till he's down, and then kicks him. He thinks they're going to go after every man in Sheldon's group, burning their property, taking their land, till they drive 'em out. . . . No, I *don't* think it's nonsense, Peg! Gil says the ATF probably knew that Richard had guns stored out there. He says they won't stop till there isn't a gun left, and when that's over, they'll take the land. . . . Well, Peg, I don't care whether you believe it or not. I tell you, Gil knows what he's talking about."

She slammed down the phone and, without skipping a beat, slammed a skillet onto the stove. "Your aunt Peg is startin' to get on my *nerves!*" she said to Ryan, as though, being Peg's nephew, *he* was responsible for her somehow. "First she goes and hires an Indian waitress, and now she's sayin' that fire at the Sheldons' was all accidental."

149

Ryan tried to connect the two in his mind. "What's that got to do with . . . ?"

"You don't see how the two fit together, either, do you?" his mother continued angrily. "It's just like the newsletter tells us—little by little they're squeezing the white race out. We're bein' left behind. Peg could've offered that job to me."

"I didn't think you wanted to work full-time," Ryan said.

"Not right now, but she could have had the decency to ask! And what's she know about the fire? She wasn't even there! Peg wouldn't know the ATF if they was to land on her roof."

Ryan's head swam in confusion. Who was right? What if it *was* the ATF who did it? What if after all this, a lot of what Gil said was true, and no one believed him? What if somebody's *house* was next?

He wanted to ask Gil, but there were still bad feelings between them. Besides, Gil clattered up from the basement in his army boots and flak jacket just then, and acted as though he had the most important job in the world to do. Maybe he did.

Charlene came to the table in her pajamas and robe and looked up when Gil stuck some bread in the toaster. He stood by the table thrusting his hand in a box of Cap'n Crunch and eating it by the handful.

"Where *you* going, Corporal?" she quipped.

"Go ahead, Charlene, laugh," he said. "Someday you won't be laughing anymore. You saw what they did to the Sheldons, didn't you?"

"The firemen said it was that old heater Matt's father keeps out there for your meetings," Ryan said.

"And you believe that?" Gil asked.

"Well, if the firemen don't know what causes a blaze, who does?"

Gil gave him a look of disgust.

"So what are *you* going to do?" Charlene insisted. "I swear, Gil, if you get your name in the paper doing something stupid . . ."

"Look," Gil said, "I'm right down at the grassroots level. I'm talking home and land and the right to bear arms, plain and simple. It's what the patriots were fighting for back in 1776. If we get local boys all over the U.S. willing to fight for home and country, the president will take notice. And if he don't, he'll wish he had."

"So where you off to, Washington?" Charlene asked.

"Just a little paramilitary training—keep us on our toes, is all," Gil said. "You think we're just playin' around, shooting at stop signs and stuff, you got another think coming." And when the toast popped, he spread both slices with peanut butter, pressed them together in a sandwich, filled his thermos with coffee, and went out.

"Gil's talking nuts," Charlene said to her mother. "Who all's he hanging around with these days? Who else is in that group besides Mr. Sheldon?"

"What do you know about it?" her mother shot back. "How do you know they might not just be right?"

151

Ryan kept out of it, pretending to read the back of the cereal box, but Charlene turned her irritation on him.

"Between you and Gil, I'll be lucky to be elected dogcatcher," she complained. "All I asked was for nobody to do anything to make anybody mad between now and March, and already you got your picture in the paper and Gil's probably fixing to."

Freddy came out in the kitchen, eyes full of sleep, hair tousled. "Are you going to be a dogcatcher, Charlene?" he asked, climbing up to get a Pop-Tart.

"Probably," Charlene said, brooding. "I can just see my future in this place. I'll end up waiting tables at Teepee's, and marry a cowboy and have six kids, and that's it."

"Well, you just put down your aunt Peg and me both with that smart remark," Doris Walker said. "Anything in this world wrong with being a waitress or having kids?"

"Or marrying a rancher?" Ryan put in.

Charlene sank back in her chair. "I didn't say there was. I just want more for myself, that's all. Something different, is what I mean."

For himself, Ryan was thinking as he rode over to Hank's later, he didn't see how there could be anything better than being a cowboy. Out in the hills by yourself, just you and the cattle, and now and then another cowboy to talk to. The clouds and the shadows they made on the land below—what could be better than that?

But what if things were changing? Already the Saddlebow was smaller than it used to be, less land, less cattle, less men. What if, when he was old enough to be a full-time working cowboy, there wasn't any place for him on the Saddlebow? What if Moe Morales's nephew came around and it was him who got to go up in the Bighorns next summer?

This much he knew: He didn't have to decide anything about the Mountain Patriots right now. He could take his time learning what Gil's group was really about; maybe he'd start going to meetings regularly, and maybe he wouldn't.

Christmas wasn't too different from any other day at Walker's Crossing. You still had to get up early, feed the horses and cattle, put down fresh hay, milk the dairy cows. Lon and Doris Walker let their kids pick out something they wanted from Teepee's or from a catalog, and there was a turkey for dinner.

There had been another big snow before Christmas, and it seemed to Ryan that half his life was spent digging out paths to the barn and the shed, if not at home, then over at Hank's. He liked to stay busy, though. Liked being out of the house.

Gil had been gone almost every weekend, and every week he looked more and more like a general— acted like one, anyway. With the Sheldons' barn gone, the men had been meeting in an outbuilding over at Big Ed's place. They bragged that the Feds may have burned the barn, but they didn't get the guns and ammo, which had been buried under the dirt floor.

Gil had taken to wearing his camouflage shirt and

pants even when he wasn't going off on maneuvers, and T. P. had told him he'd rather he didn't wear them at the gas pumps on weekends. He'd given all his help navy blue fleece parkas with TEEPEE's in red on the backs, and he expected them to wear them. Gil put the parka on over his camouflage shirt, but he still wore his combat boots.

He had put up a table-sized artificial tree in his basement bedroom on which he hung, as ornaments, little red and white nooses. Sid got them somewhere, he said, and was passing them around as a joke. Gil and his friends wished each other a White Christmas and a "Jew-Free" New Year. Ryan almost asked his dad what he thought about it, then decided he'd better keep his mouth shut. It was Christmas, after all.

"Dennis," Ryan said to the lean, gray man one evening in January, watching him shoe a horse, the horse's hoof tucked between his knees. "Do you believe everything they say about the Jews?"

Dennis Shay took another nail from his pocket and pounded it into the hoof. "What *who* says?"

"I don't know. Everyone."

"Now what in the world made you ask me a question like that?" Dennis said. "I can't hardly say I've known many Jews. Not any at all, I guess. Not to talk to, anyway."

Ryan gave a nervous laugh. "Some of it's really wild. I mean, Kevin—this guy at school—says he read on the Internet that Jews use the blood of Christian children to make matzo."

154

"Oh, come on!" said Dennis, not even looking up.

"But you keep hearing how they've taken over New York City and the government, too," he continued. "And how they really aren't God's chosen people at all—*we* are."

Shay examined the horseshoe, pushing at it with his thumbs to see if there was any wiggle, then let the hoof drop and gave the horse a pat.

"Well, now, I don't keep up with all that church stuff, but I don't guess God plays favorites. That he likes one kind of people better'n he likes another. You can sure stir up a mess of trouble with that one."

"But do you think they're trying to come out here and take Wyoming away from us?"

"There's enough land out here to buy; they don't have to *take* it. Why *wouldn't* someone want to live here? *We* do. We're not the only people in the world who like the big sky."

They were quiet for a while—Dennis examining the horses' hooves, Ryan leaning against the railing. Finally Dennis tipped the brim of his hat up so he could get a better look at Ryan and said, "What's eating at you today, cowboy? Somethin' on your mind?"

"Oh, it's just this stuff I'm hearing from Gil. About Mexicans coming in and getting our jobs, and Japs and Jews buying up our land. Like a war, almost. It *is,* sort of, because Mr. Sheldon's got . . ." He started to tell Dennis about the guns, then stopped.

155

That was probably something he wasn't supposed to mention.

Dennis, however, didn't seem particularly interested. "What it's all about, Ryan, is change," he said in his slow way of speaking, drawing out the final word of each sentence, like the slow swing of a door. "There are folks who take to it and folks who don't."

"How about you?" asked Ryan.

"Heck, I *have* to take to it. Couldn't work on a ranch if I didn't. Things are changing all the time—the kind of feed that's best for cattle, the way we plant, the way we breed. . . . The market changes every day. You got to keep your mind open to change or you don't survive in this business. New people come along with new ideas about how to do things, and you got to ask yourself, 'What can I learn from this person? What new thing can he teach me?'"

"Change isn't always good, though," Ryan countered.

"No. Reckon not. And there are some big problems—illegal immigrants, for starters. But you got to keep your eye on the big picture, and not take your frustration out on some poor soul who only wants a better life, same as we all do. Now I don't know what Gil's got himself mixed up in, but the way I see it, there's two things you can do to move yourself up in this world. The first is to become better at what you do, so you *earn* it. The second is to tear down everybody around you, make 'em look small just so's you'll look a little taller yourself." He winked at Ryan. "And you ask me, you don't need to look an inch taller than you are now."

Ryan returned his grin.

It was a subject Ryan couldn't shake off, however, since Gil was so fired up about it. So he asked Mr. Phillips one day at school if it was possible, the way Gil said, that the Jews hadn't died in the Holocaust at all—they'd died of pesticide poisoning or some horrible epidemic, and someone took pictures of all the bodies of the dead piled up and blamed it on the Germans? How the gassing of the Jews at Auschwitz was just made up, and all the Germans had been doing was disposing of their diseased bodies after they'd died.

He'd thought, too late, how angry this might make Mr. Phillips, but instead, his teacher just rested his chin on his hand and looked thoughtfully at Ryan for a moment. "I have a great-aunt who saw it," he said finally, his voice calm. "I have a cousin whose grandfather told her how he was forced to shave off the hair of the women after they'd been gassed. It was used in mattresses, you know, and pillows. I have some notes written by my grandmother that were hidden away in her cot before she died, telling what had happened before her very eyes—the way her sisters were killed. Why is it so hard to believe, I wonder?"

"I don't know," said Ryan, slouching onto a chair and pulling the neck of his sweater up around his chin. "Maybe it's just hard to think that people could do such awful stuff to each other."

"Or because some people have a need to hate," Mr. Phillips suggested. "If it wasn't the Jews, Ryan, it would be someone else. As long as we've got someone to hate, it keeps our minds off ourselves and our own shortcomings. But that's too simple an answer. I don't know why we hate. I wish I did."

That evening, Ryan went down in the basement to talk with Gil. He wanted to clear things up between them, and at the same time, he wanted to tell him what Mr. Phillips had said. What Dennis Shay had said in the barn. Just talk about it—sort things through. He remembered how, on the first day of fifth grade, when he'd found the old yellow desk waiting for him again at school and the kids had teased him, he'd come home and cried, he'd been so angry. And Gil had been kind that day. Talked to him. Heard him out. They could talk like that again, maybe.

Gil wasn't there, however. A Third Reich battle flag had been added to one wall along with a swastika, facing the Confederate Stars and Bars on another. There was a large calendar over by one window, and Ryan noticed a date had been circled in red. Two dates. April nineteenth and twentieth.

And then he noticed that Gil had penciled in something beneath the dates. Ryan leaned closer: OKLAHOMA CITY BOMBING, read the first one. And the second: BIRTHDAY OF DER FÜHRER.

Fourteen

A silence developed between them. Talking to Gil these days was like trying to reason with a skittish horse. He was either cold and sarcastic or loud and brash, and Ryan always came away feeling stupid. So he stopped trying. Dad was too wrapped up in his own worries, and Mom didn't want to hear anything bad about Gil ever.

As January became February, and February March, Charlene seemed to be gone as much as possible before the judges made their pick. Between snows, she'd be out riding the roan gelding. If she was elected Junior Rodeo Queen, she'd have to gallop around the ring showing off her riding skills and carrying the American flag, so she practiced with a towel on a clothes pole.

When she wasn't riding, she was working on lariat tricks, trying to do the overarm spin, letting the loop drop down around her arm while she continued to spin it.

"Hey, Charlene," Ryan told her. "If they make you rodeo queen, nobody's going to care if you can do rope tricks or not."

"You're probably right, but I think it's awful that nobody tells you what they'll be looking for. I could have spent the last few months working on all the wrong things."

At school she got involved in as many projects as she could manage, and liked to hang out at Teepee's on weekends where she could meet a lot of people, let them see how friendly and cheerful she was, how much she deserved to be queen.

Freddy had seemed odd man out lately. Every time Ryan looked at him, he was sitting forlornly in front of the TV, not particularly interested, but occupied. So Ryan began taking him over to Hank's sometimes, letting him sit up in front of him on the saddle, and after they reached the foreman's house, keeping him out of the way.

He liked taking his brother along, liked enclosing the small boy in front of him on the saddle, liked the way Freddy would rest his hands on Ryan's forearms and sometimes, if he tired of riding, would simply lean back, his head against Ryan's chest.

Once, on their way back, Freddy said, "I like it better at Hank's. They laugh a lot."

"We don't laugh?" Ryan asked, knowing full well what he meant.

"Not anymore," Freddy said. "Everybody's fighting all the time."

"Well, Gil gets on my nerves sometimes," Ryan told him.

Freddy thought it over. "Yeah, but if anybody tried to take our house away, Gil wouldn't let them. He wouldn't let anyone hurt Charlene, either."

Ryan grunted. "Freddy, nobody wants to take our house and no one wants to hurt Charlene. Gil's against so many people, you'd have to take a blood test to be his friend."

"What?"

"I just mean that . . . well, I'll bet he's hardly ever talked to a Jew, but he's always got something to say against them."

"Do you hate Jews?"

"No. I suppose there would be some I wouldn't like, just like anyone else, but I wouldn't go hating somebody I'd never even met."

Freddy leaned back against him, and Ryan was startled to hear him say, "Well, I won't hate them either, then. I'll even love a nigger if you tell me to."

Ryan did not go to the Sheldons' anymore, or to any of the meetings at Big Ed's. He saw Martha Sheldon once at Teepee's, and she said, "Ryan, what's happened between you and Matt? Kevin comes over, and I see Scott sometimes, but you haven't been over for a long time. Aren't you guys friends anymore?"

And when he didn't answer, she said, "You know,

Ryan, this country—the world—is at a critical time right now. All signs point to the Great Tribulation, if you read your Bible. Some people say it's coming, but Dick and I say it's already here, and what happened to our barn is just the beginning. Christian people—the *true* Christian people—have to stick together, because it's going to be a seven-year battle between good and evil, and you're going to need all the friends you've got, Matt included."

"We just don't see eye to eye on things, I guess," Ryan told her, looking away.

"Well, for Pete's sake, I don't see eye to eye with Dick half the time, but I go on talking to him. You boys have been best friends for three years. I wouldn't let a quarrel come between you."

"Yes, ma'am," Ryan said. But he didn't go to Matt's, and Matt didn't come by Walker's Crossing. At school, they ate at separate tables and barely spoke.

Matt avoided Sheila, too, and Ryan could see the hurt on her face. Sometimes when Matt walked right by their table in the cafeteria without speaking, she would exchange a puzzled look with Ryan, and then, exhaling, begin an animated conversation with someone else and let it go. Ryan and Barry and Sheila and Amy had started eating lunch together regularly. It was Matt's behavior that had given them something to talk about and, after that, Ryan discovered, they could talk about other things, too. Strange, and a little sad, that Matt had made it easy for Ryan to talk to Sheila just by staying away.

Sheila and her mother and sisters were going to Greece during summer vacation, she told Ryan at lunch one day, when the Wyoming landscape was still bleak and raw.

"In the south of Greece," she said, "in a little town by the sea where my grandmother lives, there are flowers by now."

"What will you do there?" Ryan asked.

"Visit all Mom's relatives. Eat souvlakia. Take a boat to the islands. Ride along the coast in my uncle's car."

"Sounds great," Ryan told her.

"You'd like it," she said.

That evening at dinner, he mentioned Sheila's plans.

"Well, I never had no desire to go to any of those countries," said his mother. "You can bet it's dirty. You have to be careful when you go to foreign places. The food and water can make you sick."

"Sheila's clean," Ryan said in her defense. "She's probably got the shiniest hair of any girl in seventh grade."

"Hey," said Charlene, grinning at Ryan. "Sounds like Sheila's special. Never knew you to notice a girl's hair before."

"Well, just don't make her too special," Mother went on. "I don't plan on having no Greek for a daughter-in-law, I can tell you that. If foreigners are so clean, how come tourists get sick when they go over there? Nobody gets sick when *they* come *here*."

How could she just make remarks like that? Ryan wondered. How did Mother know whether foreign visitors got sick or not? Maybe people everywhere were just immune to their own germs. He thought of all the American Indians who had died when the whites came bringing smallpox.

But Ryan's father said, "You know, I've never seen the seashore. Never seen an ocean. You'd think a man my age would have been around some, but the hills and prairie are all I know."

"*I'd* like to see the ocean!" said Freddy.

"Well, maybe someday you will," Ryan told him.

Gil hadn't been making it home to dinner some nights, and this night was one of them. He came in about nine, dirt-streaked, his boots covered with snow and mud, and was as silent as a log.

"Gil, you gettin' paid to march these men around, or you just doing this on your own?" his father asked. "You're over at these meetings more'n you are here."

"We're out in the field a lot, and let me tell you, it's no picnic," Gil said. "Trouble with these homegrown militias, everybody wants to be a commander. Sid argues with me over every damn thing, and Ed's not much better. The country's heatin' up, things are coming to a head, and every man wants to go off in a different direction."

"Well, seems you're givin' me the short end of the stick, 'cause there's a ton of work around here that needs doing. And with Hank's cows gettin' ready to calve . . ."

"Ryan's old enough to help now," Gil said irritably. "I'll be here from time to time." He ignored the food on the table, got a beer from the refrigerator, and collapsed on the sofa, reaching for the remote.

That made even Mother lose her temper. "Well, maybe just 'from time to time' ain't good enough, Gil! I set dinner on the table, never know how many are going to be here to eat it. Then you come home, the pickup full of beer cans. You guys out learnin' to protect your families, or you out drinking?"

And Lon Walker said, "If you're just a boarder, comin' and goin' as you please, maybe it's time you paid rent."

"Give me a break!" Gil growled. "We got maneuvers comin' up this month. I'll be around for the calving, but you don't have any idea that the world's right this minute sittin' on the edge, do you? Remember the 'shot heard 'round the world'? Our country's at the crossroads, and any day, any time, things could go off like a powder keg."

At school, Barry said that his dad would soon be checking out sage grouse leks.

"Yeah? He go out on horseback or what?" Ryan asked.

"No. The Department leases a plane—a single-engine super cub."

"That's what he does? Checks on sage grouse?"

Barry laughed. "All kinds of stuff. In December he went up in a chopper to check out deer and antelope

165

herds. Elk, too. He has to calculate the sex ratios—how many adult males, adult females—so they can make decisions about the hunting season come fall. I think that's the kind of work I'd like to do. I'd hate a desk job."

"Me, too." Ryan tried to imagine being stuck at an old yellow desk for the rest of his life. Cowboy on the Saddlebow was choice number one. But if Hank wouldn't take him on full-time, maybe he'd work for the Bureau of Land Management. Help decide where the ranchers could graze their cattle during the summer, and which meadows needed time to recover. Cattle *did* pollute the streams and wear down the creek banks. Ryan had seen it himself. Some people claimed cattle ate the vegetation that wild animals depended on, and that ranching was threatening the moose and elk and antelope. Maybe animals had the same kind of problems people did, Ryan thought—who should live where, and whether they could mix.

He and Barry had begun calling each other now and then, first to talk assignments, and then just to talk. Except for Teepee's and school, there weren't many places to get together, not in winter.

"You ought to come over sometime when the weather's warmer," Barry kept saying, and Ryan promised that he would. What he couldn't promise was to invite Barry back to Walker's Crossing again. Not with Gil acting like a five-star general.

Gil cornered Ryan one night outside the barn. He was as tense as Ryan had seen him. For a moment Ryan thought Gil was angry, then realized he'd been drinking.

"You see any men hanging around here—any people driving up who don't seem like they belong, asking questions?" Gil wanted to know.

Ryan shook his head.

"Anybody stop you at school with questions? Grown people, I mean?"

"No. Why?"

"You just tell me if they do."

"Hey, Gil, what's the matter? You in some kind of trouble or something?"

Gil gave a short laugh. "It's the *country* that's in trouble. It's me trying to save it, that's all."

There was a certain swagger in his walk lately, like he was full of secret information he could hardly hold in. Like the whole world was interested in what Gil Walker was up to. And probably not one trucker in ten at Teepee's knew or cared who the guy was who filled their gas tanks on weekends. But that wasn't the kind of thing you said to Gil.

The Patriot Leader arrived again from Sandpoint. This time the *Food for Thought* was: *The white race feeds the world.* Ryan hadn't planned to read it, but found himself scanning Myles A. Reddick's editorial. If a community didn't need the United States government, he'd written, they shouldn't have to pay taxes. They ran their own schools, didn't they? Their own police force? Why should they pay taxes to Washington? What had Washington ever done for them? What this country needed were more men to say no to government interference, to spread the word.

"See?" Doris Walker said to Charlene, taking the newsletter out of Ryan's hands and thrusting it upon her daughter. "It says right here that Gil's got the right idea, and you should be glad you have an older brother who cares enough to protect you."

"From what?" asked Charlene, rolling her eyes.

"From anybody who don't belong here, and would just as soon sully the white race as blow his nose, that's who. Don't think I don't know there's a family of Mexicans moved in last month, got a boy or two in high school."

"Well, if there is, they haven't bothered me," said Charlene. "Have we got any more of those peanut butter cookies? I can only have two, though. If I get to be Junior Rodeo Queen, I'm not eating anything except lettuce till after the rodeo's over."

"Ha!" said Ryan.

Mrs. Walker put on her jacket. She'd taken on the job of helping to distribute the newsletter, and when it arrived in bundles, she took them around to drop-off points where people could help themselves to it.

"I see they printed my recipe for bread and butter pickles," she said, pleased. "And they printed Martha Sheldon's prayer. *For a Peaceable Spring,* she's called it. Now I think that's a good name for a prayer. I'm going to leave off a bunch at Teepee's. Ryan, you want a ride over? Catch a ride back home with somebody else?"

"Yeah, I'll go," Ryan said.

He helped carry the four bundles of newsletters to the pickup, then slid in beside his mother, and Mrs. Walker turned the truck around in the clearing. About the only time they ever talked, it seemed, was when they rode somewhere together. Maybe the only time his mother didn't have something else she'd rather do.

"How you doin' in school?" she asked him, and he realized how forced the words sounded, as though once they took the time to talk, neither knew what to say.

"Doin' okay."

"You pull up your grade any in math?"

"Some."

A rancher was crossing the road on horseback, and Mrs. Walker edged the truck around him, then speeded up.

"Been meanin' to ask you, Ryan, about this Greek girl. . . ."

"Don't call her the 'Greek girl,' Mom. She's Sheila Harrison, okay? And there's nothing to ask. She's just a friend."

His mother didn't answer right away. Finally she said, "That's what's wrong between you and Matt, isn't it? Martha said you hadn't been over lately."

"Matt's got his nose out of joint because she's half Greek. You got to have a pedigree or something to be friends with the Sheldons, I guess."

"Sheldons are one of the finest families I know, Ryan. They want to do right by their boys, same as we all do."

Ryan looked out the window and didn't answer.

"Gil tell you he got a letter from Myles Reddick himself, congratulating him on being made commander of the A brigade?" Mother said. Ryan didn't comment, and she went on: "I think it's good that Richard Sheldon's taken a liking to Gil—teach him some things. Shows he has confidence in him." And when Ryan still didn't reply, she said, "Always seemed to me Gil just never did find himself. Figure if he ever does, he'll light up the sky."

"Unlike me," Ryan murmured, remembering how recently she had said just the opposite of him.

"Only thing wrong with you is the lead in your boots."

Ryan bristled. "I help take care of the horses, don't I? Chop the wood? I help out at Teepee's, and over at Hank's." He was embarrassed to find tears welling up in his eyes. "I know Gil's your favorite, but it doesn't mean I don't do my share."

Mother glanced over. "Why, Ryan, I don't have favorites," she said, surprise in her voice, but the pause that followed gave her away. She started once or twice to say something, and when nothing came of it, she let her shoulders slump, her hands go slack for a moment on the wheel. Finally: "Seems sometimes like you and me never did start out right. You were a breech-birth, and I tell you, Gil and Charlene and Freddy put together didn't cause me nearly the pain you did." She gave a small laugh. "It was two days before I'd even hold you. Funny, but I can remember that pain yet.

170

They say a woman forgets, but she don't. Nowadays, they wouldn't make a woman suffer like that, but I had some old horse doctor, I swear. If it'd been legal to use the come-along on me, I 'spect he would've done it."

Ryan swallowed. "Wasn't my fault," he said finally.

"'Course it wasn't, but you try tellin' a woman that when she's been in labor for thirty-six hours. . . ."

They rode a few more miles in silence.

"Seems to me there's nothing I can ever do to please you," Ryan said.

Doris Walker grunted. "You work as hard for me as you do for Hank, I wouldn't fight it. You're over there every little chance you get. There or Teepee's. Like you'd rather be there than at home."

Ryan could think of nothing to say.

At the truck stop, Mrs. Walker drove down to the end where the restaurant was and went in along with Ryan. She held up a bundle for Aunt Peg to see. "Just leaving the newsletter, Peg," she called.

Aunt Peg nodded. She had plates lined up on both arms and was heading for a table, so Mother put the newsletters on the window ledge just inside the entrance, then went back out to the truck to distribute the rest.

Ryan looked around to see if Sheila was there—she wasn't—and slid into an empty booth, just in case she *did* happen to come. Aunt Peg was checking the pie safe for a customer to see what was left, and after she delivered a piece of cherry à la mode, she came over to sit for a couple of minutes with Ryan, stopping by the entrance to pick up a copy of the newsletter.

"T. P.'s not real happy having these here at the truck stop," she said. "I'm going to have to talk to Lon about it. I think T. P. said yes just because Doris is my sister-in-law, but it doesn't make me real popular."

She reached down and massaged one ankle as she scanned the first page. "Oh, rot!" she said suddenly under her breath.

"What?"

"This stuff about taxes, I swear! It really gets my dander up. Listen, you want a doughnut? Actually, the cook just made some giant-sized chocolate chip cookies. Want one of those, on the house?"

"Sure."

Aunt Peg brought one over on a saucer, then studied the newsletter again.

"Why *should* anybody pay taxes if their community pays for everything itself?" Ryan asked.

"Because no community pays for everything itself," Aunt Peg said. "Nobody here uses the interstate? Nobody uses the U.S. mail? Nobody here gets Social Security or Medicare or calls the Department of Agriculture for advice? Gimme a break!"

Ryan felt like a straw in the wind. One minute one argument made sense, and a minute later he was thinking the opposite.

"I'll tell you something." Aunt Peg reached across the table and broke off a piece of his cookie, then popped it in her mouth. "One of the stupidest things you can do is just vote your pocketbook. I mean, make all your decisions simply on what something will cost you. I don't enjoy paying taxes any more than anyone else, but I do it. Sometimes," she added, "I wish your mom could see a little farther than the end of her nose, but don't you go telling her that."

When Aunt Peg went back to the counter, Ryan finished reading the newsletter, stalling in case Sheila *did* happen to come in.

Are you ready for The Conflagration, it asked, *between real men and the New World Order? Are you installing solar energy systems so you can heat your homes when the real patriots blow up the Jew-owned power stations in self-defense? Who will rescue the Constitution?* it asked. *The sheep people, or "sheeple," who simply turn over their guns and do as they're told, or an underground army of men who have semiautomatics hidden away in the woods, and know how to catch fish with soap as bait? Who know how to survive?*

Which side are you *on? Are* you *ready?*

Fifteen

The first of March had been as raw and blustery as Wyoming could be in winter, but by the third week, a Chinook wind blew across the range. The temperature rose, the snow melted, and it almost looked like May.

"Weather'll do that," Mother said. "Catch you off guard. And then, just when you think winter's over, it'll come at you again."

Barry called on a Friday evening and asked Ryan if he wanted to come over the next day.

"After I finish at Hank's I will," he said, not knowing yet who would drive him.

When Ryan set out for the foreman's the next day, Gil had already left the house. Ryan seemed to remember the sound of a car pulling away before it was light.

When he came back around eleven, he asked, "Gil here? Thought maybe he could drive me over to Barry's."

Dad was limping badly, and Ryan knew he'd strained something that should have been rested. There were fewer and fewer jobs Lon Walker seemed able to do anymore.

"He's off on some fool maneuver, I'd guess," Lon replied sourly. "Spends more time playin' soldier than he does playin' rancher, and my guess is he's not any better at one than he is the other."

It was the first time Ryan could remember his father talking that way.

"Your ma's takin' Freddy to Teepee's," Dad went on, pouring himself a cup of coffee. "Maybe she'll drop you off on the way."

Mother agreed, and when it was time to leave, Charlene decided to go to Teepee's, too. All four of them squeezed in the cab of the pickup. Charlene held Freddy on her lap, and Ryan sat by the door. It was a twenty-five-minute drive to Barry's house, crossing the interstate and driving over a long, flat plain on the other side. Mother was catching a cold and wasn't in the mood for an extra-long drive. She complained most of the way there, but was curious, nonetheless, about Barry's family.

"Gil says this Dubinsky fellow works for the government," Mom said, holding a tissue to her nose as they reached the house and started up the drive.

"The State Game and Fish Department," Ryan told her.

175

"Just one more agency tellin' you what you can and can't do," Mrs. Walker said.

"Mom, be nice to them now!" said Charlene emphatically.

"Of course I'll be nice!" Mrs. Walker exclaimed, her nose sounding clogged. "I'm just not up to chattin' with anybody, especially with a nose that won't give me a moment's peace."

"Well, if anybody comes out of that house, you smile at them," Charlene said. "How am I supposed to go around being friendly if I got a family of grumps? There's only three more days before they announce the winner. Last year's Junior Rodeo Queen came by the school day before yesterday and talked to all the girls who'd been nominated, and she said she'd gone around meeting everybody she could, shaking every hand in sight, didn't matter who they were. She never went out in public without a smile on her face, she said, and never would have made queen without the love and support of her family."

"Why, Charlene, we love you!" Mother insisted. "And I can be as nice as the next person. Did I ever sit any of you kids down and say you was to hate somebody? Why, if a colored was to knock on our door tomorrow and ask for a glass of water, I wouldn't deny him that."

"Yeah, but would you invite him in?" asked Ryan.

"*I* wouldn't!" said Freddy. "He might stab me."

"Freddy, you don't even know any black people. How do you know what they'd do?" said Ryan.

"I wouldn't ask him in, and I wouldn't encourage

him to stick around, because I believe what the newsletter says: Just like the birds and beasts, we've got an obligation to reproduce our own kind." She fumbled in her pocket for another tissue.

Ryan couldn't see how inviting somebody into your house automatically led to reproduction, but he owed Mom one for driving him over, so he kept his mouth shut.

"Shhh, now. Someone's coming out," said Charlene, and when Mrs. Dubinsky and Barry came toward the pickup, she called out, "Hello! I'm Charlene Walker. How are you?"

"She's my sister," Ryan explained, getting out and exchanging looks with Barry. They almost laughed out loud.

Mrs. Dubinsky was a small woman with plain features and soft eyes. She was dressed in jeans and a turtleneck sweater, and she stooped over to look in the window. "Hello, Charlene. Mrs. Walker . . . ?"

"Yes. Hello," said Mother.

"What do you think of this weather?" said Barry's mother. "John's out working today, but he can drive Ryan home later, save you the trip."

"That would be nice," said Mother. "I expect Ryan and Barry can find enough to keep 'em busy till then. You boys have fun now." She began inching the pickup forward so she could turn around. Ryan noticed that she never lingered around people who seemed different from her—people who talked differently, perhaps, or who might be better educated.

"Good-bye," called Charlene. "It was nice meeting you, Mrs. Budinsky."

Ryan cringed. "I sure will be glad when this rodeo queen stuff is over with," he murmured.

Mrs. Dubinsky chuckled a little. Then she smiled even broader as she tipped her head way back to see Ryan's face. "Well," she said, "Barry wasn't kidding when he said you were a giant."

Barry blushed, and his mother smiled even broader.

"Ryan," she said, extending her hand. "We're really glad to have you. Come on in."

The house the Dubinskys were renting wasn't any larger than the Walkers'—smaller, in fact—but the main difference Ryan could see were the books. They were everywhere. Like a library, almost.

"Boy, someone sure must like to read," he said.

Mrs. Dubinsky smiled. "We all do—all kinds of stuff. I think I'm the only one in this family, though, who still enjoys the comics."

"So what do you want to do?" Barry asked Ryan. "Just hang out around here or go to that place where I found the arrowhead?"

"I don't care," said Ryan. "Both, maybe."

"Why don't we go out while it's still sunny and come back for lunch? Want to see Dad's collection first?" Barry offered. They went into a small room that Barry's father evidently used as an office, and Barry slid open the top of a glass display case. Inside were arrowheads of various sizes, mounted on burlap, with tags pinned below telling where they had been found.

Ryan gingerly picked up an especially pointed arrowhead. He could see the beveled edge where a prehistoric craftsman had patiently chipped away the stone.

"A Shoshone?" he asked.

"Probably. Sheep-eaters, they were called. The Folsom points were used for hunting bison, the Clovis points for mastodon. We're not sure what kind I found. It's not as nice as these."

"You want me to make you a lunch, guys?" Mrs. Dubinsky called. "It's almost warm enough for a picnic!"

"Sure," said Barry. "We'll eat on the ridge."

They set out on foot, enjoying the warmth of the sun on their backs, even though the wind was still cutting, and went to the place where Barry had found an arrowhead the week before.

"What do you look for? A tip sticking out of the dirt?" Ryan asked.

"Sometimes. Or maybe you find this sort of oval-shaped clump, and you scrape off the dirt and there it is," Barry told him.

Barry had brought a rope they could use to rappel over the other side of the ridge—a twenty-foot drop—and after that Ryan showed him how to tie a loop in the end of the rope, then twirled it like a lasso and roped a piece of stump. It didn't work for Barry, but they made a game of running side by side to see if Ryan could rope Barry's feet. He could, and they both ended up in the dust.

"You're pretty good," Barry told him, brushing himself off. "Is that one of your jobs when you help out at Hank's?"

"Not yet," Ryan said. "I have to be good enough to do it from a moving horse."

They sat in a little cove tucked away on the ridge to eat their lunch—thick Texas-sized pieces of Mrs. Dubinsky's homemade bread, spread with mayonnaise and holding roast beef from last night's dinner. Also some chips, oranges, and a 3 Musketeers bar apiece.

"Your mom packs a good lunch," Ryan said appreciatively.

"Yeah, she forgot the drink, though. We'll have to hike over to the spring."

Ryan ate another section of his orange, and looked around the valley below where the clouds left irregular shadows on the fields, as though it were about to rain one place but not another. "You born in Oregon?"

"No. Chicago. That's where Dad's from. He and mom went to school there. But I don't remember it, because we moved to Oregon when I was three. Were you born here?"

"Yeah. Lived on the Saddlebow my whole life. Only thing better than living there, I figure, is owning it. I don't even know who does—a couple brothers back in Kansas, I think."

"You going to stay in Wyoming, then?"

"Sure."

"Dad says ranching's dangerous."

"Yep." Ryan leaned back, resting on his elbows.

"How come?"

"Your cinch can bust and dump you under a running horse. You can break a rein. Get trampled by a wild cow. . . ."

" . . . hit by lightning," offered Barry.

"Jiggs—he's one of Hank's cowpunchers—he's got two fingers missing. Got 'em twisted in a rope. That's one of the things that can happen to you. Or the stretcher can snap when you're pulling barbed wire, repairing a fence, and the wire coils around you. It almost happened to Dad once."

The spring was back up another hill, and when the boys finished eating they set out to find it. The water bubbled out among some rocks, clear and cold. They cupped their hands and drank large gulps. Ryan shivered as it slid between his fingers, running down his chin and neck.

They horsed around the meadow for a while, trying to find the second opening of a prairie dog's den, laughing as they waited at one hole while the inquisitive little animal popped up fifteen feet away and scolded them. Then they decided to go back and hang out in Barry's room till his dad came home.

It took longer getting back, it seemed, than it had to come up.

"Boy, you come here in June, you got to watch for baby antelope and deer," Ryan told him. "The fawns curl up in the grass and look just like a rock—just a big old rock lying there. Then all of a sudden they jump up and scare the hoot-owl out of you."

Barry laughed. "I saw an antelope chasing a golden eagle once," he said. "I think he was after her baby. Every time he dived low she was ready to kick him with her hoofs."

"They'll do that," Ryan said.

"Want to come back next week—maybe bring another rope and we'll both lasso?" Barry suggested.

"Probably can't. The Saddlebow cows will be calving, and we'll be really busy," Ryan told him. "Another time, though."

They made it up over the last rise where they could look down on the Dubinskys' house, and were surprised to see several cars in the driveway, one of them the sheriff's.

"Hey!" Barry said, staring.

A small group of people were standing out in front. And then Ryan saw Mrs. Dubinsky looking up, shielding her eyes against the sun. In the next instant she had broken away from the group and was starting toward them. At least, it looked like Mrs. Dubinsky. The woman was short and slight, with the same dark hair, the same jeans and turtleneck sweater she'd been wearing that morning, but as she drew closer, her face seemed as pale as the sky in winter.

She opened her mouth as she approached, but nothing came out. She came half running up the slope toward them, scrambling and stumbling, until Barry slid down to meet her.

"Mom?" he said, grasping her arms.

She grabbed on to Barry, dragging him down the hill with her.

"Mom!" Barry said again, his eyes huge, but she went on pulling, strange noises coming from her throat.

Ryan followed awkwardly, not knowing what he should do, what it meant. She seemed like a crazy person, not the same woman she'd been that morning at all.

At the bottom, several men in the small crowd came forward. The sheriff was talking over a cellular phone.

"Now, ma'am," one of his deputies said, "please let me take you and the boy into town."

Ryan couldn't understand. "Why?" he asked. "What have *they* done?" He couldn't imagine why the sheriff would want to arrest the Dubinskys.

"They haven't done anything, Ryan," the sheriff replied. And then, putting his hand on Barry's shoulder, he said softly, "I'm so sorry, fella. We just got some awful bad news about an hour ago. A rancher thirty miles south of here found your dad's plane. There was an accident. Somebody shot him down."

Sixteen

Ryan sat pushing himself hard against the back of the seat, feet pressing against the floor of the deputy's car as though to protect himself from impact, from what he was sure would happen next.

The dull ribbon of road stretching before them seemed to writhe before his eyes.

"Was the pilot killed, too?" Ryan asked, almost inaudibly.

The man nodded. "Dubinsky and the pilot both. There was an explosion."

Ryan felt as though he were choking. He couldn't forget how Mrs. Dubinsky kept shaking Barry's arm, saying, "Tell them he's alive, Barry! We just saw him this morning!" And Barry, his face the color of chalk, crying without making a sound.

The deputy went on: "It was out in the middle of nowhere they got him. Those shots could have come from any direction. We didn't even know he was missing till we got a call from the airport saying the supercub was two hours overdue. We figured they went down around eight this morning." Now the words Ryan knew were coming: "Ryan, would you know anybody around here who might have done this? Someone with an automatic weapon?"

I solemnly swear in front of these men as my witnesses that I will protect my country, my family, and all I hold dear to me, with my life. To the Mountain Patriots' Association, I pledge my loyalty, and in the presence of these witnesses I vow that I will never betray one of my brothers, even under torture or threat of death. . . .

And all I hold dear to me. . . . Didn't that include friends? Didn't it include Barry? Wasn't he a brother?

He felt a trickle of sweat run down his side under one armpit, the heat that was burning his neck. His hands and feet, however, felt icy.

"Ryan?" the deputy was saying.

And Ryan heard his own voice say the words he had to say: "You'd better ask Gil. He might know."

Gil came home that evening in someone else's clothes, his hair wet from a shower, his hands scrubbed clean. He sat quickly down at the table and reached for the lima beans, avoiding his father's eyes.

Lon Walker, however, wasn't eating. "Where you been?" he asked in a low voice.

"I told you where I was. Out on maneuvers. Only

we decided not to go out in the field today, so we just had small arms instruction over at Ed's."

"Whose clothes you wearing?"

"What do you mean?"

"Gil, that shirt belongs to somebody two sizes bigger'n you. Where are the clothes you had on this morning?"

"Left 'em at Ed's."

"Why?"

Gil turned on him suddenly. "I have to answer to you where my things are at?" he snapped.

The movement of his father's hand was just a flash in front of Ryan's eyes before it landed on Gil's cheek.

Gil rose from his chair like a tiger ready to spring. "You try that again, old man, you won't try it a third, I can tell you."

"Gil!" cried his mother. The family stared.

"You speak to me like that again, and you're out of this house," Lon said. "Two men were killed today, Gil, in case you don't know."

"How would I know that?" Gil said, his jaw set, hands clenched.

". . . and I asked where you *were!*"

Gil sat down again, breathing heavily. "Well, I told you." He glared around the table. "You think I had anything to do with killing someone, you're crazy."

There was barking outside and a hurried knock at the door. Gil jumped.

"Answer it," his father commanded.

Gil got up hesitantly and went down the hall. From where Ryan sat motionless in the kitchen, he couldn't see who it was, but he could hear Sonny's desperate voice: "Gil, it wasn't an ATF plane, it was a guy from Game and Fish!"

"How do you know?"

"It's on the news! Every damn station!" Sonny's voice sounded shaky.

"Shhhhh . . ." There was whispering, and the two stepped outside.

And then another sound, a car coming up the lane, more barking, the slam of a door. Lon Walker got up from his chair and walked down the darkened hall. Ryan followed. The door had blown open a few inches, and Ryan could see Richard Sheldon on the porch, facing Gil and Sonny.

"What the hell is going on?" asked Matt's father.

There was silence, and then Sheldon raised his voice. "I *asked* you! You boys have anything to do with that plane?"

"It was Ed," said Sonny hoarsely, trying to keep his voice at a whisper, but it didn't work. "He was the one said to bring it down, and Sid fired first. We thought it was ATF."

"You *crazy*? Gil, who's commander of your brigade, anyway? You take these yahoos out on maneuvers, and . . ."

"Shhhh," Gil cautioned again.

"Well, who told you to bring down a Game and Fish plane?"

"It was early," put in Sonny. "Flying low. Looked like it was coming right at us."

"You said be ready, Dick. You said it was coming to this," Gil said defensively. "But it wasn't me who fired."

Ryan, standing beside his father, saw his dad's head drop, his shoulders crumple, like air going out of a balloon.

Mr. Sheldon was talking again, his words coming rapidly, in staccato, like machine-gun fire: "Well, this is all the excuse they'll need, boys. They're going to Waco us and Ruby Ridge us like you never saw before. This might just be the spark that sets off the war. What'd you do with the guns?"

"Buried everything, our clothes, too," said Gil, his voice tight and shaky.

More noise from outside, another car arriving, and then the revolving light from a squad car rotated around the walls.

"A police car!" came Freddy's voice from the kitchen.

"Oh, my Lord!" cried Mother.

Lon Walker's legs seemed to give out beneath him. He sank to his knees, and Ryan grabbed him.

"Dad!"

For a moment his father just crouched there. Then he waved Ryan away and, without a word, slowly pulled himself to his feet and made his way back to the table.

The sheriff and one of his deputies came inside,

herding Richard Sheldon and Gil and Sonny on ahead of them. They entered the kitchen.

"Hello, Lon . . . Doris. Sorry to interrupt your dinner, but we need to have a little conference here with these men," the sheriff said. "Somebody suggested we talk to Gil about that small plane going down this morning, figured he might have a few ideas, so we're just following through."

Gil stared coldly at Ryan. Their eyes met, but Ryan didn't turn away. Charlene burst into tears.

Lon Walker rested his forehead on his hands, elbows on the table. "Gil, if you got any trace of decency left," he said, "you'll tell the sheriff all he needs to know."

The funeral would be held in Chicago, where John Dubinsky's parents lived. But the day before Barry and his mother were to leave, some of the women in the community helped Mrs. Dubinsky hold a small reception for people who wanted to offer their sympathy and what little help was possible. With Gil's arrest, neither Lon Walker nor his wife seemed able to leave the house. Lon, in fact, was having back spasms that sent him to bed, and Mother shuffled about from room to room carrying a box of tissues with her, not even bothering to shower or dress. Her head cold had taken over her whole body.

"How come those deputies drove right over here after that plane was hit?" she had said the night Richard and Gil and Sonny were arrested. "They said somebody told 'em to talk to Gil. Ryan, you rode home with one of those men. What in the world did you tell him? What did *you* know?"

"I didn't know anything! I just said to ask Gil," Ryan had told her.

"Then you shouldn't have said nothing at all! You don't know nothing, then you should've kept your mouth shut. Gil says he wasn't the one who fired that gun, and I believe him. Somebody ask you something, you just got to run your fool mouth off. . . ."

"Doris," Lon Walker had said suddenly. "Leave the boy alone."

Now Ryan waited for Aunt Peg to come by. She and Charlene and Ryan were going to the Dubinskys' together. The sky was cold and gray, the sun and warmth of the previous few days replaced by wind and snow. Ryan had no suit to wear, so when Aunt Peg drove up, she loaned him a suede jacket from Teepee's, not exactly the kind of thing they'd wear in Chicago, maybe, but it would do.

He slipped it on outside Peg's blue Ford, the sleeves an inch short, then folded himself double and slid in beside her. Charlene got in the back seat holding a Kleenex to her nose. She was grieving partly for Barry, Ryan decided, but partly for herself, because the Junior Rodeo Queen had been announced, and it wasn't Charlene.

Of course they wouldn't choose her, she had cried when she'd gotten the news. Why would they choose a girl whose one brother gets his picture in the paper standing up for Jews, offending half the population, and the other brother goes to jail, offending the rest? The only sure way to get along in this world, she had concluded, was to stay smack in the middle, don't take sides, don't get involved, just mind your own business.

Peg was silent, grave. Halfway down the drive she said, "This is sure a sorry business. I'm sorry for the Dubinskys, I'm sorry for your folks, for Gil. . . ." She took a deep breath, staring out over the road. "I'm sorry for what it's done to us . . . to the community. Except for the beating death of that gay student from the University of Wyoming—Ryan, you remember that?—Wyoming doesn't have a reputation for hate crimes, and I'd hoped that would be the last of them. Just goes to show they can happen anywhere."

"I heard them say over at the Sheldons' that that's why Matt's father came here—to get something going," said Ryan.

"Lucky us," Peg said, and fell silent again.

Ryan swallowed. "It's like a poison," he said finally. "It just creeps into a place and everyone gets sick."

"No, there's always a weakness that starts it off. Always people looking for some quick way to feel important," Aunt Peg said. "For the last three years, Gil's just been drifting, and his life's sort of got caught in the bend between high school and beyond. He never could seem to change himself, so anything else changing around him was scary. What these patriot associations are is men who are scared, and they can't think of any other way to solve their problems than to fight it out."

Walking into the Dubinskys' house, where he'd been only a few days before, was about the hardest thing Ryan ever had to do. He'd rather have a physical pain than watch Barry standing by his mom over against the fireplace, his eyes puffy, his suit coat much too big. He'd probably had to borrow a jacket, too.

Aunt Peg went first, then Charlene, but when it was Ryan's turn, he could only stand there looking down on them, swallowing and swallowing. Mrs. Dubinsky's eyes widened when she saw him, her face twisted into an expression he could not interpret. Then suddenly she reached forward and pulled him to her and, her head against his chest, said, "I'm glad you came, Ryan."

"I'm so sorry, Mrs. Dubinsky." He turned to his friend. "Barry, I don't know what to say. . . ."

Barry put out his hand, and Ryan shook it.

"It wasn't you," Barry said, his lips barely moving. "We're still friends."

Ryan didn't say much on the way home, and neither did Aunt Peg. Charlene kept sniffling from the back seat. When Aunt Peg turned up the lane to Walker's Crossing, however, she said, "You keep thinking, if you could just go back and find out how this all began. . . . Our government's done some stupid things, but the way to set things right is not to go around shooting. You've got to get disagreements out in the open. Speak your piece. Enough people agree with you, the laws'll change, because *we're* the government. We do the changing."

"You want to come in, Aunt Peg?" Ryan asked, wishing she would. He hated being in the house alone now with his parents.

But she nodded toward a car in the driveway. "Looks like your folks already got company. Figure there's enough on their minds right now without me putting in my two cents' worth."

It was a white car Ryan hadn't seen before, with Idaho license plates. Once inside, he found a stout man of about sixty with a brush haircut sitting on the couch. The man stopped talking as soon as Charlene and Ryan entered, and Mrs. Walker introduced them to Myles A. Reddick, who had driven over from Sandpoint when he'd heard the news. He merely acknowledged their presence, however, and continued the conversation:

"So that's the sum of it, far as I can tell," he said. "What comes, I guess, of delegating authority to kids still wet behind the ears. It was an honest mistake, and a tragic one, but the government's got to realize that when people can't trust it anymore, things like this are going to happen."

Ryan's father sat stiffly in his chair, large hands resting on his knees, fingers spread. "Well," he said, "I don't know what all went on at those meetings at the Sheldons', and I see now I should have made it my business, but whatever was in Gil that made him get involved in something like this, he was only encouraged by what he heard over there at Dick's. All that talk of who burned up Dick's barn, when any fool

193

could tell it was that kerosene heater he kept out there. He saw people coming at him every which way—somebody look at Dick cross-eyed, and he was the enemy."

"You can sit there and say that after what happened at Waco? At Ruby Ridge?" Mr. Reddick said heatedly. "The government gets it in its head that here's a group of people or even a family living different from the way it says they should live, and they're going to come in and break it up? The government sending in people who don't understand the land, the customs?"

Charlene began tearing up again. "I can't stand that nobody gets along," she said. "People around here didn't used to be like this, did they? When did it all begin?"

"About the time people started coming out here who don't belong," Myles Reddick said.

"Well, who doesn't belong?" Ryan asked suddenly. "Seems like *you're* the ones who can't put up with someone a little different—*you're* the ones preaching against blacks and Jews."

Mr. Reddick jerked around and stared at Ryan, as though just realizing he was there. "Why, now, you sound like you've been brainwashed, son. What I want, and what Richard wanted, is to get the government off our backs. Let the people who were already here decide what to do with their land and who can live on it. Let *us* decide who can move in and who can stay."

"Then you've got to give it back to the Shoshone and the Crow," said Ryan. "If the government hadn't moved in, the land would still be theirs and you wouldn't have an inch of it. You're just like Gil; you never did have your facts straight."

He could not believe he was talking to Myles A. Reddick this way. Could not believe he was sitting there in the middle of the room shooting off his mouth like a grown man, and his parents not saying a word. Any other time he would have felt a hand across his face, but suddenly the house was as still as a morgue, and Ryan felt nine feet tall. Nine feet tall, and glad of it.

And then Mother began to cry. Sitting there in her robe with a box of tissues on her lap and crying—the first time Ryan could remember. "I can't understand how something like this could happen! Why didn't Gil tell them not to shoot? We never hated nobody! I just don't understand."

Seventeen

It helped that the Saddlebow cows were calving. Ryan went back to school, but with Gil arrested and Hank needing every hand he could get, Ryan got permission from the principal to take the following week off to help out.

He would be glad to get away. Classmates looked at him pityingly, then stopped whispering abruptly whenever he drew near. Sheila was still his friend, he knew, but nothing was the same. Matt's mother had withdrawn him from school, to be home-schooled again, but what would happen to the family now with Richard Sheldon awaiting trial, no one could say.

The news in the paper and on TV was full of "Richard Sheldon and his Minutemen," as the reporters dubbed them. Big Ed and Sid, of course, had been arrested, too, as they were driving toward Utah, and the only way the Walkers could escape reporters was not to answer the phone or door.

Ryan stopped by Mr. Phillips' room during lunch period when the teacher was grading papers. Mr. Phillips immediately put down his pencil and didn't try to fake cheerfulness. "How are you, Ryan?" he asked.

Ryan simply shook his head and slouched in a chair, swallowing.

"It's rough, I know," said his teacher.

"I was just wondering," Ryan said at last, "what might happen to Gil. I can't even get my folks to talk about it."

"It's hard to say. The paper said that some group is trying to raise money for bail for the men, which could mean Gil might be able to come home until the trial. If a jury decides he's telling the truth—that he *didn't* fire his own rifle or order anyone else to do it—they won't be as hard on him as they will on the one who pulled the trigger."

"If . . . if the jury doesn't believe him, though, could they sentence him to death?"

"That's borrowing trouble, Ryan. If any of the men can testify that Gil actually tried to stop the firing, that would certainly help his case. But it's going to take a patient judge and jury to decide who's responsible directly for the deaths and who were accessories to the crime."

"That's almost as bad, isn't it?"

"It could be. Gil could do himself and the community a favor by being as cooperative as he can. My guess is that Sheldon's got a lot to answer for, whether he was there or not. We'll just have to wait for the truth to come out, and it's probably one of the hardest things you'll ever have to do." The bell sounded, and he said, "Listen. Come by anytime. I can come early any day or stay late if it will help."

"Thanks," Ryan said. "Thank you."

But he felt most cut off at home. It was likely that even if he'd said nothing to the deputy, they would have gotten around to Gil soon enough, and Dad understood that. But Mother was not about to forgive. It didn't help that she developed an ear infection on top of her cold. If she'd just say something out loud, Ryan thought, they could talk it out, maybe. But even when he offered to do little jobs for her, she merely grunted. At meals, she slapped his food down in front of him. Didn't make room when he tried to sit beside her in front of the TV. *As long as you live under this roof, I got to feed you,* she seemed to be saying, *but it sure don't mean I have to love you.* And Ryan wondered if she ever had.

"Where I made my biggest mistake," Lon Walker confided, "was not taking a closer look at my own son. I'd go down there in the basement, see what he had on his walls, and it seemed like a joke. I mean, the swastika—now who would take that seriously? Just Gil tryin' to get a rise out of us, I figured. But it upset

198

me, I'll admit, so I just quit goin' down there. I told myself that Gil's problems weren't as big as mine, and now I see how they swallowed him up."

As he packed his things for his week at Hank's, Ryan realized he wasn't sure just where he stood with the cowboys, either. They were a closedmouthed lot, but there wasn't a man among them who hadn't heard the news about Gil, and Ryan was afraid they might be wondering from what sort of gene pool he himself was made.

On the Saddlebow you didn't see a lot of hotshot cowboys riding around showing off. There wasn't any need. Where you showed off was in the sure way you handled the cattle, the gentle way you delivered a calf, whether you could ride out in a storm, the snow seeping down your collar, and not complain. Whether, on a long dusty ride, you'd give the water in your canteen to your horse before you'd drink the last of it yourself. If there was any bragging to be done, the other men did it for you.

What kind of a man would take an assault rifle and hide up in the hills?

What sort of a man would fight someone because of his name? His job? His religion? His race?

How did it sound that somebody on the Saddlebow was with the man who pulled the trigger? Son of the caretaker, as a matter of fact?

And who was going to trust that second son, tall and thin as a ladder, when God only knows where that gun had been hiding all along?

Ryan spread out his sleeping bag, then placed on it a couple pairs of jeans, his toothbrush and underwear, extra socks, cap, shirts, sweater, and rolled it all up. Already the boots he'd earned at Teepee's were beginning to pinch at the toes. He'd probably grown another inch since autumn, and his feet along with him. He saddled up the bay, then went back inside and got his sheepskin gloves.

"I'm off, Dad," he told his father, who was sitting in a chair by the window, a heating pad behind his back.

"Looks like snow," Lon murmured. "You're taking a week, then?"

"Yep. School said it was okay."

Lon nodded. "I know Hank's glad to have you. Tell him I'm sorrier than sorry about my back. You'll have to take over for me, I guess."

"Hey, Ryan," Charlene called, coming to the top of the stairs to say good-bye. "Leslie Overbrook's going to be the Junior Rodeo Queen, and she asked me to be her stand-in."

"Stand-in?"

"Yeah. If she gets sick at the last minute and throws up or something, she wants me to take her place. She said I might be chosen next year. Some girls get nominated twice."

Ryan grinned. "Well, don't you go feeding her hot peppers or anything before the rodeo," he said.

"Take care," Charlene told him. "Stay warm."

Freddy came over and encircled his legs with his

short little arms. "I don't like it when you're gone," he said.

Ryan reached down and grabbed Freddy's head between his hands. "You know what I'm going to teach you to do next? A little roping. We'll practice on the fence posts. You remind me when I come home."

Mrs. Walker had her back to Ryan, making a production of blowing her nose, as he said good-bye to the others.

"Bye, Mom," he said.

When she didn't answer, Lon Walker merely hung his head, and Ryan left the house.

Maybe she couldn't help the way she was, Ryan thought. Maybe some mothers just naturally loved some of their children better. He'd probably always wish he had Debbie Floyd for a mom, but this was the only mother he'd ever get, and maybe, as they both got older, she'd come to like him a little more.

The bay was pacing in her stall. If there was somewhere to go, then why the delay? she seemed to be saying, and eagerly nuzzled his neck as he led her outside.

He had volunteered for the night shift. For five or six weeks the men would put in fourteen-hour days, without a day off, but a week was all Ryan could miss of school. The rest of the time, he'd fill in on weekends the best he could.

"No!" he told Midnight and Sergeant. Disappointed, the dogs hung back.

When he got to Hank's, the day crew was coming in to be fed dinner, and Ryan realized just how much he was needed. Clyde was gone; he spent the winter months working ranches in New Mexico, coming back in time for the branding in June and staying through the haying season. Gil had always helped out before at calving time, at his father's insistence, but with him in jail, and Lon Walker laid up with a bad back, the crew was down to six plus Ryan, which wouldn't be so bad if cows all birthed during the day and no one had to check on them at night.

Dennis Shay was the only one besides the Floyds and the Walkers who lived on the Saddlebow. For most of the year, Moe ate breakfast at the Floyds' but drove home at night, to return the next day. At calving time, however, when Jiggs and Sparkie and Pete came back, Moe and the other men all slept in the bunkhouse in shifts.

An air of weariness hung over the kitchen. The room was filled with the smell of their sweat, the tobacco on their clothes, of manure and hay and grit. As Debbie once said, there was never a time you "get through" your work on a ranch. If you weren't pulling a calf, you were fixing a fence or a well, or searching for cattle in the thick underbrush along the river bottom. She herself could shoe a horse or cut a calf with the best of them.

"Ryan, you eaten?" she called, turning a thick slab of ham over in the skillet.

"No, ma'am, but I can go right out," he said, wanting to appear useful. Eager.

"You sit down and have a bite, then you can go to

202

work," she said, unsmiling, and Ryan obeyed. She was probably tired, too, he thought, but still he wondered: Had she changed? Had they all had a change of heart toward him?

Sparkie was the only one who mentioned Gil's arrest. "Durn shame about that brother of yours," he said, but not so loud it carried over the whole kitchen.

"Yeah," was all Ryan could think of to answer.

Hank and Jiggs and Pete formed the day shift. Dennis, Sparkie, Moe, and Ryan were the nighthawks, as Debbie called them. The twelve hundred expectant cows were penned in two fifty-acre lots, the three hundred heifers in an adjoining thirty acres to one side. Contrary to most of the ranches, the Saddlebow liked to keep a very young-aged herd because of the rough summer pasture, but the huge number of heifers made calving time extra busy. The day before, Hank had discovered that a section of fences had been trampled, and the heifers, who often needed help in birthing, were all mixed up with the cows. There was no time to separate them now, because the calves were beginning to come.

"Whatever can go wrong *will* go wrong," Hank said, explaining the situation to Ryan.

Every hour, a cowboy or two would ride through the drop pastures, checking to see that all was well, driving the heifers ready to calve into the calving sheds. If a heifer didn't give birth within an hour or so after being put in a stall, the cowboys would pull the calf from her. Usually they used only their hands, their arms encased in plastic sleeves, but sometimes they attached chains to the slippery legs of the calf just to get a better grip. Only if the heifer was in real difficulty did they use the come-along.

Both Debbie and Hank looked weary. Debbie, wearing her old down jacket and boots, helped out in the calving shed when she could, but had the task of feeding the men morning and night when she'd rather have fallen into bed herself.

Hank had his eye on the sky. "Wouldn't you know the temperature to drop?" he said, shaking his head. "Seems that winter's staying longer and longer each year. You'd think we'd be over the worst of it by now."

"Not by a long shot," said Jiggs, reaching out with his fork to spear the last piece of ham, only to collide with Sparkie's fork in midair.

"I'll go halves with you," said Sparkie, grinning sheepishly.

"Remember when we had that snow in May?" Jiggs continued, looking at Hank.

"Yes, but a May snow, it doesn't stay around long," said Moe.

"Heck, Moe, all we need is snow two inches deep, and it's already up to your knees," Pete kidded, and everyone laughed, Moe included.

Dennis Shay took a long drink of coffee. "You young pups aren't old enough to remember, but there was an April storm back in seventy-two, I think it was. Why . . . that blizzard rode in here and carried off more'n two hundred fifty new calves. Another in eighty-three, it froze two hundred fifty thousand sheep and cattle in the state. The big die-up, we called it. If you're a young rancher with a small herd, and a storm carries off half your cattle, it's good-bye to the big sky. The young ones, they'll leave Wyoming fast as they can catch the next bus."

"I want every new calf that's dropped tonight brought into a calving shed with its mother," Hank said to the others. "Don't leave any out, no matter how healthy they look. Don't just bring in the calf, bring in the mother to nurse it. We get a heifer that won't nurse, then we got to play nursemaid. Debbie's got the formula ready out there, and Shay, you inject the calves with caffeine, they're looking down. We got the infrared lamps in the stalls, so we're ready. Let's try not to lose any."

Although it was ordinarily only four hours till Ryan's bedtime, he felt that staying up all night would be no problem at all. He was charged with adrenaline, and wanted only to be on his horse.

The first night he went out with Dennis. Sparkie and Moe went immediately to the calving sheds to check on the calves that had been brought in during the day. From there they would go to the north lot to make their rounds of the birthing cows, while Dennis and Ryan got on their horses and began a slow patrol of the south lot, looking for heifers ready to spill.

Despite the sharpness of the wind, Ryan thrived on a job on a horse. Any job. He loved to feel the swells of the saddle against his thighs, the slight stretch and give in the stirrup leathers. And he loved the company of Dennis Shay.

It was the first time he'd been asked to stay for a week—first time it was acknowledged he was staying overnight, in fact, sleeping with the cowboys in the bunkhouse. He was hardly conscious of the rain on his face until it turned to sleet, pinging against the reins and saddle. The bay mare plodded along with her head down, unmindful of the beams of their flashlights as they scanned the ground to the front and sides of them, looking for a heifer going off by herself, away from the herd, or, if she were in trouble, trying to lie down on her side.

Barry would have loved coming along on something like this, Ryan was thinking. He was easy with horses. He could learn. No matter what happened, he decided, he was going to stay in touch with Barry Dubinsky, wherever the guy moved with his mother. Oregon, probably. If Ryan didn't slip up here at the Saddlebow, and if they let him hang around during the summer, he was going to ask Hank if Barry could come too. Maybe Mrs. Dubinsky would let him fly out, glad to have him spend a summer on a ranch. Then again, maybe not. . . .

At the same time, he couldn't help thinking of Matt. They'd meet now and then, he was sure of that, unless Mrs. Sheldon, with a new baby on the way, moved her family back to California. Ryan wanted to plan in advance what he was going to say. Something like, *Listen, Matt, I don't believe in the Mountain Patriots anymore, but whenever you want to come over. . . .* Nah.

Matt, your dad was dead wrong about. . . . No, that wasn't it, either. Well, something about how they'd had a lot of fun together, and would always go on being friends. But maybe that wasn't possible. Maybe Dick Sheldon's arrest would turn Matt more in the same direction, because his dad's predictions had seemed to come true.

Dennis slowed his gray gelding, placing his flashlight between his thigh and the saddle for a moment, and reached down inside his jacket for the tin of Copenhagen in his shirt pocket.

"You get all fifteen hundred cattle delivering in a six-week period of time, Ryan—you figure, well, that's about two hundred fifty calves per week, right? Say one hundred twenty-five calves in the north lot, one hundred twenty-five in the south. One hundred twenty-five calves a week divided by seven is about eighteen births every twenty-four hours, less than one an hour. That's not bad, you think. The cows can pretty much take care of themselves, and we should be able to handle the heifers, even if we have to pull each calf. Right?"

He laughed as he tucked a pinch of snuff between his lip and cheek and thrust the tin back in his pocket. Then he put on his glove again, and picked up the flashlight.

"But you've got three, maybe four hours without much happening at all, and then, it's like popcorn in a popper. Every kernel starting to pop at once. You got heifers delivering here, calves comin' out there . . . they don't line up orderly like, and take their turn.

And dirty . . . ? There's nothing polite about a cow, I'll tell you that."

Up ahead was a dark blob that looked at first like a large bush but, on closer inspection, was a heifer in the act of spilling. She stood near the fence, turning her head from time to time to inspect her hind quarters, where a light wet sac was beginning to emerge beneath her tail.

Shay handed his reins to Ryan and got down off his horse, but they kept a respectful distance.

"You're doin' okay, girl—nice and easy, that calf's coming out a perfect package," Shay murmured.

Again the heifer strained, a soft lowing issuing from her throat, and again she jerked her head toward the emerging calf.

Then suddenly the sac was spilling out onto the ground. The mother twisted around to smell it, push it with her head, inspect it, it seemed, to see whether or not it was hers, and then immediately began the work of biting off the sack, her teeth pulling at the tissue so her baby could breathe.

"Now there's a heifer with sense," said Dennis. "Goal here is to get the calf up on its feet and nursing. As soon as you see it's okay, you nudge that cow and her calf back to the calving shed. Once you get 'em inside and that baby nursing, you start out again."

Dennis rode off to inspect the rest of the lot, and, once the calf was able to remain standing, Ryan set to work urging the heifer and her new calf back toward the long, low shed where other heifers were nursing their young.

Who could not love being a cowboy? Who could not marvel at a moment like this, when a single wet sac turned into a new life, right before your eyes? Ryan began talking to the heifer to soothe her, to get her used to the sound of his voice. He slowly turned his horse's head and began guiding the new mother to the calving shed where fresh hay waited.

The calf protested at first—bawled when the heifer moved away—but with Ryan's gentle prodding, it followed its mother along the frozen ground and into the warmth of a stall, and Ryan set out again to catch up with Dennis Shay.

It was a night of waiting, then hurrying, then waiting again. They rode in overlapping circles, far away from the north lot where Sparkie was keeping vigil. The sleet had stopped temporarily, but the wind had picked up, and when the rain began again it came as snow—soft, large flakes floating down to cover Ryan's thighs, his arms, his gloves—to frost the bay's head and mane.

When dawn broke, Ryan was ready for sleep. He and Dennis Shay sat exhausted in the calving shed, their gloves drying over the potbellied stove, waiting for the day crew to come in, the smell of wet wool and leather mingling with that of straw.

Dennis tipped his head back against the wall, eyes half closed, and gave Ryan a weary smile. "First day of calving, you feel like you're about as tired as you can get. Second day, you discover it's not true, you can get a whole lot more tired than that, and by the end of the first week, you know you never was as tired in your whole life. You take six weeks of that, Ryan, bringing new calves into this world, introducing 'em one by one to Wyoming in the spring and, tired as you are, you wonder how anyone could not love this life. You wonder how anyone could sit at a desk in some concrete building somewhere and not honestly rather be out here."

He let his eyes close for a minute or two, and the way his head jerked, Ryan knew he had actually fallen asleep for a minute. "And then," Dennis went on, "you understand that this life ain't for everyone. It takes all kinds, and you're sort of glad of that—that they *aren't* all out here, crowding the land."

"Barry Dubinsky's dad loved it, too," Ryan said, remembering. "Barry told me his dad hated desk jobs— he was so glad when he got this job in Wyoming."

Dennis silently shook his head. "I didn't know him, but the fellas at Game and Fish said he was a fine one—fit right in, easy to get along with. And then . . . somebody to go and take his life. . . ." Dennis let out his breath and sat up suddenly, slapping his thigh. "Let's go in and see if that thievin' day crew left us anything for breakfast."

Again, Ryan told himself, the unfinished sentence, the unspoken thought. He had the feeling that he would go the rest of his life not knowing how Dennis and the others felt about him, that nothing important would ever get said.

Eighteen

It was the second day that they ran into trouble. Ryan was learning to tell when a heifer was about to spill her calf. Sometimes she'd lie down, then get up again. Or she'd leave the herd and go off by herself. He was glad when he could get her to the calving shed. It was safer to birth them there, out of the wind and snow, where there was warmth and light and milk at the ready if she refused to nurse her calf. But on this second night, an exhausted heifer labored without result, lying on her side and huffing.

Ryan watched as Dennis removed his heavy jacket, his sheepskin vest, his denim shirt, the flannel shirt he wore over his long johns. He rolled up the sleeve of the underwear above his elbow. Getting down on his knees, he worked one arm up into the cavity of the animal, his eyes half closed, lined face intent. Arm muscles straining, he began to back up, inching his own body along the straw and, as his hand emerged, Ryan saw that he was grasping the feet of a calf, gently working them out of the body of its mother, his arm covered with blood and manure.

"What you have to remember, Ryan, is to time your pulls with the heifer's pushes. You don't just reach in there and pull against her. But when she pushes, and you feel her body bearing down, you got to be ready to help her out. Now," he said, "you take over."

"What?" said Ryan.

"Go ahead."

Ryan took off his jacket and got down on the straw beside him. Dennis taught him how to study the cow's sides, watching her body to know when she was pushing, straining. Ryan put one hand up inside her along with Dennis's to feel for the calf's head, and Dennis guided his hand, showing him what to feel for, how to tell which way the calf might be situated—where and when to tug.

And Ryan delivered his first calf.

He sat back on his heels, thrilled to see new life there before him. His clothes were stained with the messiness of birth, but he didn't care. This was as raw and real as it could get, he knew—there was nothing between him and life—he had reached in and grasped it, and there it was. The little calf reminded Ryan of a jackrabbit, with its big ears and funny long legs. He panted as he sat back and watched the heifer lick her baby.

Ryan was so tired when he went in for breakfast the third morning that he could not talk, could hardly seem to chew, he was so weary. Fatigue was the common denominator in the Floyds' kitchen. Debbie herself looked about as unkempt as Ryan had ever seen her, and pushed half-fried slabs of French toast onto the table for the men to help themselves. She had to get out there to the calving sheds, there were babies to attend to. These men, she seemed to feel, could fend for themselves if necessary! Ryan's mother said she'd be over to help with the cooking as soon as her cold let up, but meanwhile the men had to eat.

"I'd get me another man to help if there was any to be had," Hank told Debbie, "but every man around here I'd trust already has his hands full at one place or another, and anyone I wouldn't trust, I wouldn't want touchin' my calves."

Moe at last talked his wife into coming for a few days to help in the kitchen, while the grandma tended her babies at home. Now the food had a little more spice and zing than it did before, and it seemed to suit the men—gave them more energy. The dark-complexioned Carmen smiled constantly. Cooking for men was a nice change for her, and Debbie was clearly grateful for the help.

Ryan worked, ate, slept; worked, ate, slept . . . Day rolled into night and night into day. When one of the cowboys took up his bedroll from off the rusty springs of a bunk, Ryan simply unrolled his and went to sleep, sometimes in everything but his boots. And his boots, when he pulled them on again in the mornings, felt damp and cold. There was a shower, but often there simply wasn't time to take one. The bunkhouse smelled of unwashed bodies and especially of unwashed socks, but Ryan was too tired to care. He got up when Hank or Dennis told him it was time, and went to bed again each day after breakfast.

Ryan was dead tired when he crawled in his sleeping bag, yet woke numerous times during the day, awakened by all sorts of things he wasn't used to hearing when he slept—the slam of a door, the shout of a ranch hand—so that by evening, when it was time to roll up his sleeping bag and let one of the day crew have his place, he felt light-headed and groggy.

On the fourth evening he awoke to snow. Real snow. Not only snow, but frost on his bedroll, and wind shrieking around the windows of the bunkhouse.

"We got ambushed by a blinkin' blizzard!" Pete told him, giving his shoulder a shake.

"And what do you bet all the cows will get to calving before the day's over, every durn one of 'em dropping at once," said Dennis.

Ryan still had to get used to eating chili and corn bread or steak and potatoes when he woke up, and breakfast just before he crawled into bed, but it seemed the last few days as though his body was running on automatic, and he simply moved in rhythm to the work.

In the Floyds' kitchen, Hank looked worried. "Forecast is six inches, would you believe? I don't want any heifer spilling out there in the snow if we can help it. Long as they've got food, a cow can stand the cold, but those new calves won't last long in a snowstorm. They don't eat in the first two or three hours, they're done for. Bring in all the heavies whether they're calving or not."

The men stoked up as though they wouldn't eat again for a week.

"Heck, Ryan. Your feet, they stick out so far over the bottom of the bunk, I could hang my hat on them," Moe told him, reaching for the bread. "And look at this! I eat twice as much as you, and don't grow any taller."

"It all goes to your belly, Moe. Maybe if you'd tighten your belt another three notches before you start to eat, the food wouldn't have anywhere else to go but up," Jiggs said, and the men laughed.

The windows were steamed up, the smell of wet wool overpowering. Outside, the landscape was a blur of white—a whiteout, they called it. Ryan couldn't even see the barn and bunkhouse, much less a lone animal about to spill. He had never heard the wind howl quite so fiercely, as though winter knew that this was its last chance, and had been mustering all its reserves for now. When he started out, Ryan tried shining his flashlight straight ahead of him, but got only swirling snow and a fog of white beyond.

He had been paired this time with Moe, and didn't like the way Moe nudged his horse a little ahead of him, rather than riding alongside the way Dennis had. It may have been because the snow was deep, and he was making a path for Ryan to follow, but Ryan resented it. Didn't want Moe getting the idea that Ryan needed help or that he couldn't do the work, and that they needed the Morales nephew around the ranch next summer.

He nudged his own mount forward until it was on the flank of Moe's horse. The bay gave a snort of annoyance, nipping slightly at the pinto.

"Hey! Don't crowd me, Ryan!" Moe said.

Ryan pulled back without saying anything.

As Dennis had predicted, there were more heifers ready to spill or already in the process of dropping their calves than there had been any night yet. Ryan didn't know what was going on in the north lot, but in this one the bawl of one calf seemed to be followed by another farther on, and their mothers were camouflaged by an inch of snow on their backs. The bay whinnied and tossed her head, protesting the cold, the dark, the snow balling up under her hooves.

"Ryan, only way to do this, we got to split up," Moe yelled above the howl of the wind. "You listen to me, now. Long as we're out here together, I'm the cow boss, see. Don't you go anywhere you're not following fence. You can't see fence, you stop till you find it again. You follow the fence on around and come back. Bring in any heifer and calf you find along the way. If you get out there in the middle, we might not ever find you. You understand?"

Ryan nodded. He'd be glad to go off by himself.

"Hank's not even going to bed tonight, and Debbie's out there with him. I'll go back and forth across the lot, bring in what I can. If we lose a calf, I don't want it to be on my watch."

The force of the wind snapped Ryan awake if he wasn't before. The snow, half ice, stung his eyelids, made an icy crust on his clothes. Already Moe was bending over a newborn calf struggling to get to its feet, and Ryan noticed the way he simply hoisted it over his shoulder and, with the mother mooing and lowing behind him, led both her and his horse back toward the calving shed.

Ryan rode on, shining his light ahead of him, but he did not get far before he saw a heifer—her body heavy—needing to come in.

Hour rolled into hour, one trip out became another, then another. He changed horses, saddling a sorrel. Twenty minutes later, along the west fence, he found a heifer lying on her side in the snow, huffing with every push, it seemed, but somewhere up ahead, he heard the bawl of a newborn calf, and decided to tend to that first.

"We're trusting you to check the fence line," Dennis told him when Ryan came in with the new calf and its mother.

"I am," Ryan told him.

The cell phone in Debbie's coat pocket rang, and when she answered, Ryan could hear Jiggs's voice: "We got trouble over here—one of the older cows. I think she's just too weak to push."

Debbie rested her head on her arms, exhausted. Hank reached over and rubbed her neck with one hand, picked up the phone with the other.

"Where you at, Jiggs?"

"'Bout as far off the planet as you can get—up the back of the north field, near where the spring used to be. Better bring the come-along."

"I'll be over," Hank said.

A cow who had given birth to a stillborn stood lowing helplessly in a neighboring stall, her udder distended, waiting to nurse. Debbie was inoculating the calf Ryan had just brought in, and Sparkie came in with still another. Both the day and night crews were working.

Ryan bundled up and went back out again, comforting the sorrel, giving him an apple as a treat, then started along the opposite fence to see what he might have missed the first time around. The wind let down, then surged again, and just when he thought the blizzard had done its worst, it returned with a screaming encore. The horse's white mane seemed to disappear before his eyes.

He had been moving along the east fence when he suddenly remembered the heifer across the lot, the one on her side in the snow. He should have gone back to her at once—should have started this trek over there, not here.

One of the other men will have found her by now, he told himself, and then he remembered Shay's words: *We're trusting you to check the fence line,* and he pulled back on the reins, his stomach tightening.

He tried to think how far along the other fence from the calving shed he had been when he saw the heifer—when he'd passed her by to take in the new calf and its mother. About twenty minutes, he remembered. By his estimate, he had been out now about fifteen. Perhaps he was almost directly across from where the heifer had been trying to spill. If he followed the fence line all the way back to the calving shed and started up the west fence from there, it could take forty minutes to get to her. But if he was right—if he was almost across from her now—he could, if he crossed the lot, get there in ten or fifteen minutes.

He turned the sorrel toward the center of the field and shone his light again. But still he hesitated.

The snow was swirling, making cotton of the air. There was no moon at all, no stars. A wilderness of white between him and the other side.

I'm cow boss tonight, Moe had said. *And you stick to the fence.* . . .

Had he given that order because it was necessary or because he liked to play boss? Ryan wondered. If it was so dangerous getting out there away from the fence, why was Moe doing it? Was this just his way of taking over?

Ryan let out his breath, agonizing. He should have gone right back to that heifer. If she'd dropped her calf, with the snow coming down on her baby. . . . And if she *hadn't* spilled yet, she was in trouble. . . .

He pressed his knees against the sides of the sorrel, jiggled the reins, and the horse moved forward.

Nineteen

He kept the light shining steadily out in front of him, as though the beam were the needle of a compass, pointing the way. He checked his watch by the light: 2:47 A.M.

"Just a few more hours to go, boy, and you get a warm barn and fresh hay," he told the horse, but the sorrel only snorted, his head jerking forward with each reluctant step in the deepening snow.

Moe did not need to find out that he had left the fence, and if Ryan saved the heifer's calf, it would be worth it. There were times you had to think for yourself, no matter what—situations where old rules didn't apply.

The huge lots where they kept the cattle were

rectangular shaped to fit the valley floor. On a clear day, you could easily see from one side to the other, width-wise—make out a moving cow, anyway. In the dark, of course, you could see nothing, and in the snow, less than nothing, so how long would it take to go across? Once he got to the fence on the other side, he'd turn right, because he estimated he'd be short of where he'd seen the heifer. He hoped she'd be on her feet and nursing by now.

There were no landmarks to help chart his path. Every snow-covered clump of sagebrush looked like every other. The mountains, which would have helped in the daytime, were replaced by the blackness of night and the whiteness of snow.

Inescapably, as though if his mind did not worry him about one thing it would trouble him over another, he thought of Gil—Gil and Big Ed and Sonny and Sid and Mr. Sheldon, the five of them—off in a jail somewhere. He wondered if Gil was asleep right now or if he was looking out at the storm and the dark, and thinking how there might have been a time when he had made a decision, as Ryan had tonight, to go right or left, this way or that, to follow the rules or make his own, and whether or not he was sorry.

Impatiently Ryan held the light up a little higher, thinking he should have seen the opposite fence by now. Either the snow was coming down harder or the light was giving out, or both, because the beam was growing dimmer. He pulled up his jacket cuff and shone the light on his watch: 3:22. He should have reached the fence long, long before this. Not only had the wind picked up, but the temperature must have risen a degree or two, because the snow was no longer soft. It felt like slivers of glass on his eyelids. Sleet again. The sorrel tossed his head, hesitating a time or two as though awaiting further instructions as to whether he should keep going straight ahead. Ryan didn't know. All he could do was press his legs against the horse's sides and urge him on.

Five minutes later, when there was still no sign of the fence—when, in fact, the light had gone out entirely—Ryan felt the cold, hard taste of panic in his throat. He could no longer see his watch. No longer see the land. No moon, no stars, only a swirl of night about him, the huff of the horse's breath in his ears, the ping of sleet against his cap, the saddle . . .

All the stories of blizzards past came rushing in like demons to torment him: travelers who were found frozen to death just over the hill from a motel; men who had lost their way and were found frozen only ten yards from their own woodpiles.

He let out his breath in shaky exclamations and, in panic, turned the horse to the left. The sorrel went obediently, as though he were glad someone knew where they were going. But after a few minutes of plodding, Ryan panicked again, and turned the horse to the right. The horse snorted and whinnied, but shook himself and obeyed the command.

Ryan felt the cold now. He was colder than he had ever been in his life. Colder than the time he and Matt had stayed out on the bluff, taking turns on the new snow saucer, and he'd almost frostbitten his toes. Colder than the time he'd been in the sleigh when Hank took hay around to the far ends of the holding lots, and Ryan had tossed it out to the hungry cattle. He would have given anything for hay right then to bury his toes in. If he had hay, he would stuff it down the neck of his jacket, never mind how scratchy it would be.

If Moe was crisscrossing the lot as he'd said, maybe he'd find him, but Ryan hated to think what he'd say. How could Ryan explain why he had disobeyed? To save the heifer, of course, but wasn't there something more? Something about the name Morales, maybe? Something of Gil inside himself?

He was hungry, but all he could think about was warmth. If he were offered food or water or straw, he would take the straw. The cold numbed his face, his fingers. It seemed to have numbed his brain. How long had he been out here trying to cross? One hour? More? It was as though the boundaries of his world had all gone skewed, as though everything he had counted on before was up for grabs. Nothing was sure.

The sorrel suddenly whinnied again and stopped, and Ryan leaned forward in the saddle, trying to see if they had actually reached a fence. What he could make out in the whiteness of snow was a large black clump on the ground ahead, and . . . numbly, woodenly . . . he climbed down from the saddle and went over to check.

It was the heifer, the hoofs strangely extended, the body stiff. Between its legs was the half-delivered body of a calf. The calf, too, was dead. And beyond them both, within a few yards, in fact, the fence.

Ryan's legs went out from under him, and he knelt down on one knee, head in his hands.

If he had not forgotten the heifer, but gone right back to her . . .

If he had—two hours ago—retrieved his steps instead of trying to cross the lot . . .

He had lost not only the calf but its mother. With the stress of the birth, and then the cold, her heart gave out.

Ryan knew the way now to the calving shed but he didn't want to go. Didn't want to face the men, especially Dennis and Hank.

Looks like we put our trust in the wrong person, Dennis would say. No, Dennis wouldn't say anything, and that would be worse. He'd just study Ryan like a piece of unfamiliar meat on his plate, and push it to one side without comment.

Ryan was too cold, too numb, to get back in the saddle. Taking the horse's reins in his hands, he led him along the fence, and the sorrel trotted on a little quicker, perhaps sensing the direction they were taking, his white tail swishing in anticipation. Not fifty yards farther on, an abandoned calf stood bawling, trying to nurse from its mother, who kept turning her body away. The calf's legs were giving out; it was almost too weak to stand.

Just like human mothers, Ryan thought, maybe some heifers were born to the task and some were not. You either took to it or you didn't, and you couldn't make a mother love you any more than you could make her nurse her baby.

Eager to have something to show for his efforts, he struggled to pick up the calf as he'd seen Moe do, draped it over his shoulder and, holding its hind feet against his chest, his other hand holding the reins, he followed the fence until he saw the light from the windows of the calving shed.

"Ryan, where have you been? We were about to send a search party for you!" Moe exploded as Ryan came in. Then he saw the calf. "Now that is a sick one," he said.

Ryan nodded. His eyelashes were coated with ice, his lips so numb he could scarcely speak. "It's m-mother wouldn't nurse it. F-found it out by the fence on the west side."

Debbie pointed to the straw beneath an infrared light, and Ryan put the calf down. She covered it with a blanket and thrust the nipple of a large bottle into its mouth.

But Dennis was studying Ryan. "You see any others out there?" he asked. "You go the whole perimeter of the fence?"

Ryan stood motionless. He could lie. He could say yes, he'd been the whole perimeter, and he'd come upon that one heifer in trouble, and he'd done what he could, but couldn't save her. He *had* to lie. His future depended on it—next summer at the Saddlebow.

His eyes met Dennis Shay's. *We're trusting you,* Dennis had said.

"I didn't go the perimeter," Ryan said, his tongue thick. "I made a big mistake."

It was worse than his seat at the yellow desk had ever been, the whole class looking at him. The others' eyes were on him now, Hank's and Dennis Shay's most of all.

"When I brought in a calf earlier, I'd seen this heifer on her side not far away, and figured I'd get back to her. Then I forgot." Ryan stood in the middle of the floor holding his cap, which dripped melting snow down onto his boots, scuffed and stiff and dirty. He could only stare at them. "When I went out again, I started up the fence on the east side before I remembered." He paused. "I should have followed the fence right back and gone around, but I was afraid I'd be too late, so I tried to cross the lot and didn't make it in time." Moe gave an exclamation. "My light gave out," Ryan continued, "and I must have been circling a long time. The calf's dead, and so is the heifer."

"The heifer, too?" Hank said. He swore under his breath and looked away.

Nobody else spoke. What was it Mother had said about Ryan once? *Give him an idea and he has to run with it—try everything that comes along.*

Maybe she was right. Maybe he didn't have what it took to be a cowboy, much less a cow boss. He'd been given one simple instruction to follow, plain as the nose on his face, and he hadn't even been able to do that: *Just stick to the fences. Follow the fence. Don't try to cross the lot.* . . . An idiot could have done that. Put Freddy on a horse, and even Freddy would have followed through.

"Ryan," said Debbie finally, "I'm so tired, I'm about to drop. You brought this calf in, you got to tend to it." She gave him a little smile and patted his arm as she passed.

Grateful for something to do, Ryan took the bottle from her hand and straddled the calf while it drank, holding it fast between his legs. The men wordlessly began moving again, each to his own task.

He had thought he was too tired now to care, too cold to think, but as he felt the calf weakly suck at the nipple, Ryan thought of where he'd be come summer, and knew it would not be up in the Bighorns with these men. It would be Moe's nephew who would come, do a man's work, and end up in the Bighorns, and why not? He'd have earned it.

Ryan would end up at Teepee's, pumping gas. Probably T. P. would let him work the pumps now that Gil had been arrested. It was better than nothing, a better job than most of the guys his age had. *You either take to ranching or you don't,* Dennis had told him. Translated, *You've either got what it takes or you don't.* Maybe it was harder to change what was down inside you than you thought. Maybe it wasn't as simple as a single yes or no.

As the calving shed emptied and men set out again for their rounds, Ryan was surprised, almost grateful, to find that he was overwhelmed with fatigue. With sleepiness. An escape, he imagined, from humiliation.

The calf lay down and was drinking more vigorously, but its body was shaking, and Ryan wondered how long it had been out there, how much sooner he would have found it had he been where he was supposed to be. No one else had been checking along the fence line because that's where Ryan was told to go. They had trusted him.

He took off his jacket and wrapped it around the calf, tucking the ends under like swaddling clothes. Then, reapplying the bottle to its mouth, he lay down behind the animal, curled up against it as though they were spoons. He rested his head on one hand and, with the other, continued to hold the bottle.

From time to time he found himself drifting off, holding the bottle too low for the calf to drink. Then he would shake himself, tilt the bottle again, and prod the animal to suck.

Men came and went, heifers were led mooing in from the cold. Ryan got up once, refilled the bottle, then came back, relieved to find the calf breathing still, its body warm. He put the nipple to its mouth again, but didn't remove his jacket from the animal. He covered himself with straw and once again curled his long legs, his arms, around the calf, becoming one with the animal. And once again he slept.

This time he slept in earnest. He dreamed that he and Gil and Dad were all out in a field together looking for calves, except that the snow was gone and his dad could ride again, and it seemed more like a vacation— the three of them going somewhere together. In the dream his shirt was open, and he could feel the breeze on his chest, his arms.

Then he was conscious of being cold, and when he opened his eyes, the calf was gone. Dennis was sitting on an overturned milk can, holding Ryan's jacket.

"Better put this on," he said. "It's cold."

Ryan tried to rouse himself. There was straw in his hair, and his mouth was dry. "Where's the calf?" he murmured. "Did it die?"

"No. I just put it in the stall with the cow who lost hers. Didn't think she'd take to it at first, but it started nursing, and after a while I guess she decided it could stay. It's got sturdy legs. I think it'll make it."

Ryan let out his breath, relieved, and sat up, thrusting his arms in the jacket. He started to stand, but Dennis said, "It's okay. Things have slowed a bit. We can afford a rest."

"Looks like I took more than my share," Ryan said.

"You've been incubating that calf," Dennis told him, and then he looked away. For several minutes neither spoke. Finally Dennis said, "You know, Ryan, Hank and me have been at the Saddlebow a long time. We've had some good men here we've had to let go, much as we wanted to keep them."

Ryan sank back against the wall and stared at his hands. He was glad he and Dennis were alone, that there was no one else to hear.

"Had a man up from Austin once," Shay went on, "probably the best wrangler we've ever had. Rope a calf standing on his head, if he had to. But Hank let 'im go 'cause he couldn't be trusted."

Will they even let me stay the rest of the week? Ryan wondered. Did he have to face the humiliation of going home before his time was up?

"Here's the thing," Dennis said, "there's not a man or woman alive who don't make mistakes one time or another. Sometimes a big one. That fella from Austin, for example. He'd leave a gate open and first thing you know we were losing cattle. And 'stead of 'fessing up, he'd leave us wondering did we have a poacher? How long had the gate been open? A day? A week? Should we try to count all the cattle in case we had a big-time rustler who had pulled in with a truck and driven off with a load? Hire a range detective? A simple confession would have saved us a lot of grief."

Ryan swallowed.

"Now you take tonight. You could have told us you stuck to the fence and had gone all the way around. That the heifer was dead when you first found her, the calf, too. And we would have taken you at your word, nobody be the wiser."

Dennis Shay's eyes met Ryan's. "But you told it like it was, so we went out there to check the perimeter, the way you should have done, and found three more calves down at the far end. If you'd lied, if you said you'd been around and hadn't seen a one, we'd never have known they were there and might have lost them all."

Ryan waited without breathing.

"It takes a big man to admit he's done a fool thing, Ryan, and your dad was such a person. It'd take him a while, maybe, but by and by he'd say, 'I'm wrong.' Gil? Gil always took the easy way. Wanted to ride without the work; be a boss without any idea in this world what it means to be a man. You're a long way yet from being a cowboy, but Hank says there's no better way to learn than to eat, sleep, and breathe cattle, and looked to us like you were doing a whole lot of that tonight."

He was forgiven, then.

And Dennis said, "Moe and me will be taking the cattle up in the Bighorns in late June this summer, the weather cooperates. We'd sort of like to have you along, make you a part of the crew." He winked at Ryan. "Figure we'd be the only cow company in Wyoming with both the tallest and shortest cowpokes in it. That ought to be worth somethin'."

Ryan could only stare.

"But . . . I thought . . . Moe's nephew . . ."

"Haven't even met him yet. But if we need him and he earns a place on the ranch, I expect the Saddlebow's big enough for both of you, don't you figure?"

"Sure!"

He could hardly believe it. Visions of summers to come stretched out before him—summers turning to autumns, and autumns to winter snows. Roping, branding, riding, calving . . . sun, wind, snow, and— finally—the sweet-smelling rains of spring. All under the most beautiful sky in the West.

When he didn't answer, Dennis said, "That is, if you can stand the smell of cowboys' feet for three months straight."

Ryan began to smile until a grin took over his whole face. He couldn't stop it. He gave a yip of delight, and then a small yell, startling the cattle.

Dennis laughed, and so did Ryan.

"Oh, man! They'd smell like clover to me," Ryan said. "Tell Hank I'd like it fine."